HER DARK ROSE

DARK SPELL SERIES BOOK 7

ISRA SRAVENHEART

CONTENTS

DEDICATION

I give thanks and the most humble gratitude to all those who have inspired me and the events that inspired the Dark Spell Series.
Every single word has a sentiment that cannot be described in words so all I will say is thank you so much!

To Sam,
who remains a remarkable spirit.

And last of all, to the real Astrid,
who has made this series all the more real with his strong energy, generosity, inspiration and we can add love in there for good measure.

1

Many believe death to be the end. But what if death is only the beginning of something else? I'll have to elaborate on my meaning. We must go back to a time long ago, a time when a witch reigned supreme. She was both good and evil. Yes, she was both and she had no qualms about being both. She loved the darkness of the night. She admired the beauty in the twinkling stars. She also loved the light and brilliance of the sun.

It was black as night. A tall tower looked radiant in the distance, like a mountain that stood alone amongst the rest. A white figure could just barely be seen looking out of a window. She was dressed in white, and she was a vision. When you looked closer, you could see her long, white hair with delectable curls that framed her face and danced down her back. Her dress was torn with three harsh slashes across her stomach. This figure was Lady Isra.

She hadn't been seen for many moons. Many thought her to be perished. Even her lover Astrid believed she was no more. He grieved, mourning her tragic passing. It was a somber scene with ravens all across the land gathering in their hundreds, coming together in that poignant moment to pay respects to Lady Isra of the Dark.

However, there she was, standing by the window, alive and well dressed in the ensemble that she had supposedly perished in. The tears across her dress marked the event, as did the scars on her skin where ice blades had sunk deep into her flesh.

So, what had happened? Did she die? Or was she saved from some unrecognizable force? Whatever it was, it was evident that Astrid knew.

The question remained as hours after her alleged death, Isra was able to breathe, and Astrid gasped as her life force magickally returned. Only one question stood in his mind: was she still immortal after such an event? He now feared she could be killed and that an attempt on her life would be made again.

He had gone away on a quest to find an answer. He wanted to know for sure if Lady Isra was immortal as she had always been, or if she was now mortal. Her restoration wasn't that important to him but finding out whether something like this would occur again was a much more worthy cause.

Astrid had been away on his soulful quest for three painful months, painful because he needed and missed Isra. He felt the hurt deep within him. It tugged at his heartstrings as each day passed without her. He so wanted to talk to her, but he also knew he had to be mentally strong.

Being away from Isra would ensure that nothing disturbed his focus in his important task. He felt that if he was alone, he would think better even though being away from his love was pure torture. He couldn't wait for the day when he would find himself in her arms again. He relished her touch. Just wanting to hold her and not being able to was harsh on him. It cut him deeper than he could imagine.

2

The winds brought a great chill and the open window invited the cold air in. The late afternoon sun was slowly fading as a dreary grey filled the skies. The figure in white knew the day was coming to its end.

Isra looked at the vast image before her. She let her eyes delicately climb the immaculately placed hills, admiring their beauty. She then maneuvered away from the window. Her eyes sparkled as they took one last glimpse of the picturesque scene.

But what had become of the rest of the tower's inhabitants since Isra's fated death? Well, not long after Isra died, the freezing spell placed upon Contessia and Klinq miraculously came undone. This was not typical behavior for a spell, but in this case, circumstances prevailed.

It had left Contessia and Klinq dazed and confused. They had awoken from it, not knowing why they were there and with no memories of what happened prior. All they could remember was their hatred. It lay among them like a corpse, thanks to Cora's spell. Contessia eyed Klinq with contempt. She didn't want him around her and felt suspicious in his presence. She no longer trusted him.

Astrid materialized soon after and informed Contessia that she

3

was to return to her bedroom for the time being as Isra was unavailable. He was stern and harsh as he commanded her to vacate before he turned to the gnome with contempt, proceeding to deal with him in a firm manner.

This only caused Klinq to wonder what Astrid had in store for him as he stood face to face with the raven-man in that dingy, damp basement cell. Fear penetrated the air as Klinq awaited his impending fate. Astrid didn't waste any time as he banished Klinq from the lands in the name of Lady Isra.

The raven-man had seen to it that the gnome had a thorough reprimand. He warned Klinq that if he returned, dire consequences would follow! Astrid was satisfied Klinq had taken heed of his stern warning, knowing that if he returned, the price Klinq would pay would be far greater than anything he'd ever known.

Contessia felt great relief when she heard about this, though she became confused as to why Isra wasn't present. But Astrid was cold, refusing to answer any of her questions. Contessia was unable to roam the grounds of Shambre Fell as she pleased as per Astrid's instruction. He told her she could never leave the tower because although Isra was indeed gone for the time being, her soul still belonged to Isra.

Isra turned away from the window and looked back at the room around her. The infamous couch had disappeared and now there was just a vacant space. An elegant, gilded gold chair sat at the back of the room covered in rubies and emeralds and in place of the couch, a round oak table matched with four antique chairs could be seen center stage. Gracefully sank into the gold gilded chair, her arms majestically embraced the strong built arms. She turned her attention to a roll of pages placed beside her on her left. She picked them up, unknowing of what the contents would reveal.

She began to read the pages, letting her finger rest on the first page. She let out a shy giggle. It was a letter. She never got letters, so she found it intriguing to receive such a thing. Her face began to show a smirk. It beamed across her entire face. The content deeply amused her. Her laughter grew loud. She reveled in the joy the words gave her. She laughed once more as she placed the pages down.

Now what could have made her so engulfed with amusement?

She allowed the letter to replay in her mind, her emotions expanding as each word danced as she perused the page. The letter was from the council, more precisely the people in charge of magickal matters behind the scenes. Isra fondly remembered the council well from her days in training where she had also met her recently vanquished foe, Everilda.

The council wanted to speak with Isra in person to discuss some perplexing concerns they had, particularly over Astrid's recent behavior.

Isra laughed when she read the paragraph referring to Astrid. It said, "...the raven whom you decidedly made into a human, despite knowing that such things are commonly known to be met with dire consequence."

Astrid had grown into a fine man, dealing with his shift from raven to human in a most splendid way, she thought with a wild grin on her face. Just the thought of Astrid in his human form, standing so solemn and bold, did more for her than anyone could ever know! But she kept those indiscreet thoughts to herself.

She glanced over at the letter again, noticing the just about decipherable date that had been scrawled so thoughtlessly. It revealed that a visit was scheduled for tomorrow. Isra laughed again. *Oh, this should be intriguing,* she thought.

Isra gave it no more thought and discarded it from her mind, hastily lifting herself from her seat. She maneuvered herself to the window ledge, planting herself upon it. Her eyes shifted as she watched closely. Black skies were slowly being tinted with fragments of light. It was soon to be morning.

Astrid appeared in her thoughts as she looked upon the lavish landscape in front of her eyes. He must be lonely, she thought, noting the longing she felt, a longing she felt from him, pulling her to his side. *He must be projecting a need for me to be near him,* she thought to herself. She did miss him although she understood he would be back when he was ready.

~

IN ANOTHER REALM beyond the bright, full moon amidst the stars, Astrid was comfortably sat up in a lavishly furnished bed dressed in white silk sheets with embroidered delicate roses on the curtains surrounding it.

Astrid's whereabouts were unknown as he had kept his destination as well as his mission a closely guarded secret, even from Isra. He was on a quest in an unknown land where he would remain until he got what he was seeking.

As it was late in the night, Astrid was drinking a very hot and delicately sweetened coffee. He felt something strong and pulsating circling all round him. It was driving him crazy, but he wanted more. He felt it entering his mind and surrounding his soul. It engaged his sensitive feelings. He simply couldn't pinpoint this energy, but he had an inkling it was connected to Isra.

Ah! Isra. *His* Isra. What could be said about her? He had been separated from her for many months now. They hadn't broken up or parted ways, but he had taken it upon himself to go on a mission to discover if she could be harmed or killed in any way.

He had almost lost her, and it devastated him, but before he could discern what had occurred, Isra was breathing again inside the warm safety of his arms. He couldn't believe it. He was overjoyed! His eyes filled with tears of happiness and relief. He had almost lost his love, but fate prevailed and restored her to him.

But only one question lies in wait ... why was she restored after her untimely death? She should've been taken to the deepest depths of Hell because those who are dark eventually find themselves in Hell. He knew this to be true for some, although he didn't understand the complexities of it. He believed Hell to be a place that one lived in unaware.

Astrid had many beliefs and philosophies, but he understood the darker ones best. He didn't completely understand Isra's dark ways or know much about them, but he had embraced her dark path and walked alongside her. He wanted to know everything about her and so her magic was now a part of him.

He paused, finishing the last of his coffee. It seemed sweeter than usual although he couldn't fathom why. He was sure he hadn't added any sweet ingredients to his favorite blend but in these small hours, he felt an extra surge of sweetness, almost as if someone had sent some very powerful energy source in his direction.

Astrid couldn't lie; he liked the sweetness but he couldn't figure it out. He wondered if Lady Isra was experiencing the same. He wanted to talk to her but he knew now wasn't the right time. The event would commence when they were ready, but whether it be hours or days was simply unknown.

All Astrid could do was be patient, for much greater things lay in sight when the day came for him to return!

3

young man stared intently at his reflection. He had just come of age. His ash-blonde hair, cut perfectly, showed off his sideburns as he preened himself ambitiously with a fine-toothed comb. He felt like he was over-doing it with his preening and fixing up of himself, but he had a lot to be proud about. He wanted to look his best for whatever came his way and being the smart young man he was, he knew there was a lot to come.

Ronald O'Kutte was in his prime for a mere nineteen-year-old that had the entire world at his feet. He had come to a great milestone in his life and the glory was going straight to him. It was a consequence of the loss of a family member, his brother Kane.

It had been two years since the disappearance of Kane, so now Ronald was about to take the role of warrior and leader of his village which greatly pleased him. It was not clear how Kane O'Kutte disappeared, but just before he'd vanished, he'd boasted how he was going to find a witch and become all powerful in her name, telling great stories to whomever would listen of how he would finally have all he'd ever wanted by having access to such power.

Ronald shook his head when he heard the story. He knew his brother was reckless and lacked thought, so it was no surprise to him when many days passed where no one saw Kane. Those days soon turned to months and years.

Ronald's father had a stern talk with him after the two-year anniversary of Kane's disappearance, as some feared his death. The family had taken it upon themselves to grieve although they had not wanted to give up hope for the boy.

The father was firm, insisting Ronald should take over as warrior when he reached nineteen years of age. It would be a good few years before the honor would be bestowed to him. This shocked and both surprised Ronald as he wasn't expecting to have such responsibility at this early point in his life.

Ronald's dear father, Charles O'Kutte, sadly passed away shortly after this insistence. He was old and infirm and ultimately the disappointment Kane had brought upon the family had worn the old man down. The poor man was heartbroken. He suffered greatly as his weak heart gave up its ability to beat.

Ronald was now the only man in the family. There was another brother, but he had his own life with a maiden quite a distance away from Spindlevitch. Nobody had seen or heard of him in years. Ronald remembered his name but that was all.

With Kane missing and both of his parents deceased, Ronald took it upon himself at his tender age to be the man he had always wanted to be. He knew what he needed to undergo in order to achieve his dreams. He didn't berate himself, nor was he unrealistic about his expectations. He knew life was hard.

Ronald discovered he had a keen interest in the occult. He wouldn't dream of telling the other villagers though. He kept vigilant, keeping his interest secret.

He wasn't a warlock, but he had been studying the metaphysical world. Magick wasn't his original pursuit in life, but since magick had so violently dominated his family, he was curious. He was also cautious. While Ronald had his reservations about magic, he knew he needed to find the source of it while on his quest. That source was Lady Isra, the witch that Kane had sought out with hopes and plans of world domination.

Ronald didn't know much about Lady Isra, but he deemed her solely responsible for his brother's vanishing act. Ronald wasn't about to follow in Kane's footsteps; no, he had a much better plan.

Isra was not aware of Ronald or his plans, but he was soon to make her aware of him in the most unexpected way.

4

Araven circled the skies. The early morning rise of the sun made its appearance as he passed through its orange and yellow rays. He felt almost blinded by the colors. Plundering ahead but motivated as he pursued his destination, he emerged into the clear blue light of day.

He paused for a moment as a silhouette of a tall tower standing on a hilltop became the focal point of his left eye. He was careful, surveying the majestic building with his mission in mind as he prepared to swoop down for a landing. His eyes now feasted upon the tower as he prepared to enter the home of Lady Isra.

The mysterious raven had long planned his journey to get here. He'd heard of her a long time ago and now he had finally arrived at his destination. Silas had meticulously drawn up everything to the last detail. He planned on staying for a while to assist the witch as best he could if she allowed.

As he perched upon the window frame, he did not transform into a man, so he was not Lady Isra's counterpart, Astrid.

One could assume he was from another land. He was well mannered in his attitude and endeared in his appearance, humble enough to accept what is and embrace it. This raven was much different to Astrid in terms of his personality. He had a spiritual outlook about himself, and it showed. He wanted some of that outlook for Lady Isra, although he knew her heart lay in the dark arts. He was going to try his best anyways; for he knew light was the key.

As Silas peered beyond the window, he saw Lady Isra abuzz in her own pragmatic world and engrossed in a mindset of productivity. The sun blistered through all of the windows, allowing every segment of light to come bursting in. She admired the natural look of the place; it added something different she hadn't noticed before. Of course, she hadn't allowed a single drop of light to filter into her dark fortress for many years. Now that was changing.

Today was going to be an intriguing day for Isra. She was expecting guests, a rare occurrence in her home. The council was going to be meeting her there today to discuss what they viewed as important matters. Lady Isra didn't see the need for importance, but she was going to allow the meeting to take place in any event.

She wouldn't have to heed to their advice as she knew she would continue to reign supreme. Whatever they said she would take with a pinch of salt. After all, what power did they have over her? They were just a council, and she was a fully-fledged witch in her own right.

Silas silently watched Isra as she busied herself with getting everything ready for the council's arrival.

Isra was preparing a fresh pot of tea for the day's festivities, orange tea she had made herself. She wanted something more refined, but it would have to make do. The council had finer tastes and she knew it, but they would have to adapt to her natural way of things.

She wanted to be ready for what they would be relaying to her, though noting that she didn't have to pay it any mind. She suspected the entire meeting was going to be a reprimand anyway and therefore imagined her raven lover would emerge in the debate as it was all about Astrid.

Silas watched Isra as she dressed a round oak table with a cloth of white silk, adding a vase of delicate white lilies. Normally, this color wouldn't be one she would choose of her own free will, but she decided to allow it just this once to show elegance, trying to embrace the formality of the occasion.

Silas stopped at once, hearing a noise from below. Maneuvering himself back onto the window ledge, he peered downward. He was shocked to see a man appear in the grounds, standing by the ornate door. This unknown man was keenly peering through it silently before whispering something into the antique keyhole and quietly letting himself in.

But before he closed the door behind him, he turned around, making sure nobody knew he was there. Silas pondered the question, why was this man being so quiet? There was a creepy feel to him although the raven couldn't fathom why. The man seemed normal in appearance, but something about him made the raven uneasy, like someone that would emerge at the most inopportune times.

The man entered, slowly gliding up the staircase and delicately tracing the rails as he maneuvered himself to the center of everything, the place where Lady Isra would be right at that moment.

Silas was on tenterhooks watching it all and observing the act being conducted by the man. Did he need to make himself known to the witch and reveal to her she had an intruder in the tower?

He sat quietly as he awaited some sign to let him know what to do. He hoped he wouldn't have to attack, but he would if he felt the need.

The man lingered beside the main tower room, softly and gently making his way in. Silas noted that the man had carefully engineered his arrival so that his visit would come as a surprise.

The man smiled, knowing Lady Isra had no inclination of his arrival, and he decided to keep it that way. The man was Astrid, her lover, unbeknown to the fellow raven that had no clue as to his identity and was wondering just who he was and whether he needed to swoop down on him and give him what for.

Astrid wanted Isra to find him unexpectedly. He hadn't told her he was coming home and he had high hopes for her to be surprised in a most pleasant and endearing way. He paused, knowing his act could cause shock for her as he hadn't given her a time on when he would be home, but he remembered that she loved him, so all would be okay.

Astrid grew nervous when he thought about his approach. He remembered the last time he'd seen Isra. It had been a few hours after the paranormal phenomenon occurred where she had mysteriously been restored after death. Isra was in the dark about the truth of that. Only Astrid knew and he was keeping tight-lipped.

Isra, frail and weak in her early days following her resurrection, sprang nervous, a quality in her that Astrid hadn't known before. She wasn't normally one to be frightened. Heck, she was frightening. It was in her nature as a dark being. Astrid saw through all that though and knew deep down she had fears. She was insecure. She worried about things. He knew it all.

He had surveyed her carefully. Her emotions seemed to be connected with a great intensity, surrounded by fear. Astrid noted it in her body language when he saw her standing in front of him as he prepared to say goodbye. She looked as though she was about to dash away from something, and he could see it inside her. The intensity of it made her dark heart beat faster. It took over her body. She was ready to go. She put on a brave face, but inside she was terrified. He could see it although she said nothing.

Astrid was calm as he explained that he needed to go away for a little while to seek something out. He was cryptic in his wording. He didn't want Isra to know the exact details. He didn't want to cause her any worries and so he'd made it seem like a quest to figure something out about himself, which it wasn't.

Now he was about to be back in her presence. He couldn't help but wonder how she would react after not seeing him for such a long time. The absence had been killing him spiritually. He had wanted to return much sooner, but alas, much work had to be completed before the reunion could take place.

Astrid paused as he reached the top of the staircase, positioned by the door that would lead him home. Gently allowing his fingers to slowly grasp the door handle, he pressed down and took a deep breath before he moved his hand away. He was nervous about seeing her but he wasn't going to let that show.

Silas, who was still in his position by the window, could no longer see the man Astrid and was not sure what to do. He felt anxious as he wasn't sure if this man was dangerous, but it was clear why he was here. He was watching Lady Isra, as was Silas. Both Astrid and Silas had keen interests in Lady Isra although neither of them knew what the other individual's interest in the witch was.

Silas watched with a keen eye as Astrid slowly entered the room. Astrid was quiet as he opened and closed the door, ensuring it shut silently behind him. He was careful as he snuck up behind the witch, placing his hands on her neck, ready to steal her away for a passionate, sweet kiss.

Isra was in a midst of thoughts as he played out his motion, so she did not immediately notice him. Her mind was busy and elsewhere and so Astrid smiled as he seized upon his chance. Astrid was clever. He used his hands as he pounced on her, covering her eyes so she could not see him. She was initially startled, feeling a tremor that shook deeply within her.

Astrid breathed on the nape of her neck while keeping his hands in place over her eyes. She felt his breath. It made her writhe with ecstasy. She had a good inclination that it was him. Only he could be touching her in this way, but she proceeded to giggle, saying nothing. There was only one man who could provoke such exhilarating feelings in her. That man was Astrid.

He clutched her tightly. He wasn't going to allow her the chance to run away. Isra shuddered slightly at the intensity of the interaction they reciprocated for one another in such synergistic cooperation. Astrid smoothly slid one of his hands up Isra's dress, cautiously making sure she was still in his firm hold.

His thumb and fingernails daintily caressed her back slowly and gently until he reached the small of her back at which he stopped, looking at the area of her skin that was beautifully exposed to him and pressed his lips against her valiantly. He had pressed upon her his delicious kiss whilst concentrating on the texture of her skin, still holding onto her tight.

He whispered softly in her ear, "I'm home. Kiss me."

"Oh Astrid!" she exclaimed, feeling emotional.

A small tear left her eye ducts. Nothing more needed to be said. She felt him. The feeling coursed through her body as she felt him all over her.

There was only one way Isra could have responded to his romantic gesture. She turned and grabbed his neck, swiftly pulling him to her so she could see his face, the same one she hadn't seen for so long. She then glanced into his eyes.

He noted the emotion in her, although now there was something new. Something very significant. Astrid held her close to him and he stared deep into the abyss that he found inside those emerald green eyes. They were like oceans. Deep in the green hues of her eyes, he could see the wilderness beyond. He could see her entire soul. There was not a thing she could have withheld from him.

She didn't hold anything back from him, she loved him, but he knew something was different. He thought maybe almost dying had changed something in her. Maybe she had to die a little inside in order to feel again. He didn't verbally explain the thought, and instead he kept it in mind.

Finally, he spoke. "I'm glad you are comfortable with my reappearance," he said, feeling relieved as he loosened his grip over her slightly, letting the anxiety inside him go.

She straightened her stance, allowing him to hold her again. "Of course, I am comfortable. What peculiar idea gave you the impression I wasn't?"

She was curious as to why he was so anxious and on edge. He was normally bold and confident. Nothing would faze him! She couldn't fathom why he was such a hot mess all of a sudden. He looked at her as if he feared she didn't want him anymore. Astrid was such a perplexing man at times, and she found him difficult to figure out even though she felt she had known him for many lifetimes.

"I don't know," he answered.

He appeared sheepish, looking down at the floor, avoiding her question. He knew he should have been more confident, but alas, this anxiety had been crippling him. He kept a brave face because he believed as a man he had to. He hadn't always been a man, but since he was one now, he wanted to be the best man he could be.

Isra glanced at the clock; it was almost ten! It was nearly time for the council to arrive. With Astrid's arrival and romantic interruption, she had totally forgotten they were coming!

Oh, how silly of me, she thought.

Astrid noticed her train of thought as she glanced at the clock. He didn't like it and thought something was wrong.

She turned to him at once, noting his worry and smiled. "The council is coming here today. They want to discuss some concerns with me. They mentioned you in the equation," she uttered regretfully, knowing he was a private man and wanted his life to be very much confidential, unless that person was Isra.

Astrid looked bothered now. He had a personal preference that his life with Isra was to be very separate from the rest of the world. He didn't feel ashamed of her as people and beings knew he was in her life; however, he didn't want it to be a focal point of discussion.

"Why do they want to discuss me?"

He frowned as he posed the question to her. He hated when those who didn't know him critiqued his life in such a way. He found it intrusive and disrespectful.

She answered with deep regard for his concerns as she mirrored his frown. "They don't agree with my transforming you into a human and you staying here with me. They state that such things go wrong with dire consequences!"

This remark made Astrid chuckle. *What dire consequences?* he thought. *We met. We became great friends. I became attached to her. She set me free by allowing me to be with her in the same form that she lives and breathes in. What could possibly go wrong? It sounds like they don't understand love.*

But Astrid understood love quite well. Love was the very thing that had brought him to this point. He understood it more than anything. He also knew the pain of it. It hurt. It was strong although intangible and couldn't be broken.

"Oh, very well. Let them do whatever they feel they must," he retorted, still feeling the urge to chuckle at their pathetic lack of integrity and respect. He knew at once that whatever was spoken about him at this meeting, he would not be happy with, and he had every right not to be.

Isra noted his touch of amusement and wondered why he was now amused about the situation when only a moment ago he seemed so cross! Again, the complexities of Astrid puzzled her. He had a split personality in a sense.

Although he never showed a harsh side towards her, she knew he could be a very vindictive and also violent being when he desired. The mind games he had played with Contessia and his trickery and coldness in his manner of speaking to her was cruel, but again, it was a side of him she would never have to experience. In a ghastly way, she admired it. She relentlessly enjoyed that he could match up to her and that they both could be in this dark way but not turn on each other with it. She felt good about that.

"Well, they will be here any moment." She sighed.

Astrid noted her dreary tone and said, "I think I will make myself scarce, if you'll pardon the expression."

Isra smiled. "That was exactly what I was hoping you would do."

She paused, staring out of the window and watching for the council leader and some of his members who would be arriving very soon. Isra turned around to see Astrid in his raven form swooping upwards to a bookcase.

Perfect, she thought. *Just in time.* "Hopefully, they will not be here long!" she murmured.

"They had better not be. I want to get my hands on you and while claws are fine things, they cannot deliver kisses," Astrid mused as he landed on the top of the bookcase, sitting in silence like a dormant statue.

5

Astrid cawed loudly as his beady eyes caught sight of a group of people in black robes heading toward the tower. From his idle spot on the bookshelf, he had a good view of the council members and could see them, but they would not be able to catch sight of him.

"I think they are here," he said.

Isra sighed again, turning her attention back to the window. Astrid was right; three figures dressed in black were making their way toward the tower.

"I suppose I'd better greet and let them in. Here's hoping they won't be staying long!"

Now that the room was silent, Silas reemerged from the window ledge, peeking in again. Silas wasn't aware that Astrid was in his raven form, nor did he have the knowledge that the man he had witnessed was one of his own kind. He didn't want to miss anything but he knew that now was not a good time to introduce him. Lady Isra not only had a man for companionship whom Silas didn't know, but she was expecting uninvited guests! Silas would have to wait to make her acquaintance.

Isra opened the window and she leaned over the ledge, almost knocking Silas over and flying from the edge. He was amazed Isra didn't catch him there and then, but he quickly flew away, hiding behind the corner.

The witch peered out, watching the figures as she muttered, "It's the love and light brigade."

Her eyes watched them all but the leader was the one who had her attention the most. His name was Magnus Zul Wingdom. She imagined it would be him doing most of the talking today, or maybe drawling on would be a more accurate description.

Isra did her best to picture Magnus Zul Wingdom from memory, trying to remember his appearance from when she had known him. He was an old and stuffy man with a pompous, high and mighty attitude. It was a shame the same thing couldn't be said for his mane of impetuous black hair that collided down his neck in a strange fashion.

Magnus had scolded her on numerous occasions for having too many temptations toward the black arts. He had told her she should be learning the lighter side of the craft but his words fell on deaf ears with young Isra. She had been in her early teenage years when she was under his wing, and even then, she found him irritating. Now that she was older and more powerful, she wasn't going to tolerate any nonsense.

Isra chuckled heartily as she remembered when the stuffy leader got turned into a measly earthworm by her old foe, Everilda. It wasn't his favorite moment, but it was highly entertaining for Isra.

She had remarked at the time, "Ha, it couldn't have happened to a nicer man!"

She had also ridiculed Everilda for it, knowing that only a terribly pathetic witch could muster such poor magic. Yes, even years later, Isra still never let Everilda forget that fatal mistake.

Isra made haste as she dashed down the magnificent staircase. Her hands collided fiercely with the rails as she swiftly rushed down. She had dashed down so quickly she felt a little out of breath. If she were being honest, she was a little nervous. If she had any other way, she'd have made it impossible for them to come. However, the council had power just like her and like other things in life, she simply had to deal with it.

As she reached the ornate wooden door, she paused. She wasn't sure if she wanted these humans in her home. She wanted to make them feel unwelcome. *It's too late for indecision now,* she thought. *They are here.* Isra knew they would discuss every single ghastly thing they didn't like, criticizing every detail, sighing and huffing with disgust at her, but eventually they would go away.

The meeting had been sprung upon her rather thoughtlessly, but she felt it had been designed to catch her off guard. In her mind, that was a fruitless effort. She had nothing to hide. Neither did Astrid, but she would defend him to eternity. She'd had a feeling that she'd come under fire sooner or later for her romance with Astrid.

The council had always strongly advised against transforming an animal into human form because they felt like and asserted very clearly that things could go wrong with serious consequences in the aftermath. And it didn't matter whether love factored into it or not. It was strictly forbidden. That was the way of things.

Of course, Isra didn't play by the rules. She made her own.

Magnus Wingdom sipped his tea while peering at Isra through his small-framed glasses. He had been sitting there for a few minutes and was almost ready to start their deep discussion, one that would piss Lady Isra off. He knew she'd find fault with what he was saying, but he had obligations to the universe.

Isra sat calmly poised with her tea on the table beside her. She had been maintaining eye contact with the pompous oaf. She was going to defend her union with so much resolve that there would be no fighting her. She was bold in her approach. She was also rather feisty, so dimwitted Magnus would have a tricky job undertaking what he was about to do.

He had brought some friends along with him. Isra knew them all very well from her days as a student in the coven. The first was Lady Vama Coheart, Isra and Everilda's teacher. Isra fondly remembered Lady Vama as someone who would do their best to teach the student an important skill but would completely fail to explain the logic and reasoning behind it. Isra felt that Lady Vama lacked real world knowledge and that maybe, just maybe, she wasn't as well rounded in the field of magic as her credentials suggested.

The other companion Magnus had brought along for the ride was his dearest and most trusted friend, a fellow professor, an owl named Otto Jinx. Otto was a most renowned teaching professional at the coven and despite her reservations, Isra had the most paramount respect for him.

There was one mystery guest among the intriguing selection of personalities, a young man with dark blonde hair. He couldn't have been any older than eighteen years of age and boasted a pale complexion with eyes as blue as the sky. He sat next to Lady Vama inquisitively as he listened to the forage of voices that wanted to be heard today.

Lady Isra paid him close attention as he surveyed her. She wondered what his interest in magic was. He smelt mortal to her and came across as an observer. He was inexperienced, that was clear. He had a great willingness to learn and that was widely shown to Isra.

Magnus began to clear his throat. He held some handwritten scrolls in one hand, a pen in the other. He would be taking notes throughout the course of discussion, Isra observed.

"Lady Isra. We are here today to discuss concerns the council has over you and some interactions with others."

He paused, taking in some more of his fragrant orange tea. The scent was so potent Isra could smell it from across the table. Isra maintained her focus.

"I see," she retorted, pushing her empty teacup aside. "Well, go ahead. Say what you must!"

She put on a small albeit false smile. She wanted this over with already! It was getting irritating!

Magnus Wingdom got straight into it, his voice uttering sounds that resembled a moral high ground and perhaps also a lack of introspection. Isra surveyed him from her distance across the table.

"We have a few concerns over this raven that you so rashly turned into a human. There have been several incidents noted regarding this 'man's' behavior. You see, the council has laws and morals regarding the universe and this man, this Astrid as he is known, is hazardous to say the least."

"I see. And may I ask what business the council has with this?" Isra fiercely inquired.

"He's menacing in dexterity and his knowledge of the realms is deadening."

Isra let off a small cackle, feeling as though she were unleashing steam from the very root of her. "So, I presume the council would prefer Astrid to stay situated in his raven skin?"

"That is most undoubtedly correct," Magnus acknowledged.

Isra laughed again. "Astrid will stay in his raven and human forms, free to switch between them as he chooses. I am the one who created him for the masterful soul he is and it is only when my soul is dead and incarnated that he will become trapped in his outer raven exterior. Until such time, Astrid will remain a man," she declared.

Magnus questioned, "So you admit you cast the spell that gave him his masculine body?"

Isra looked at Magnus, noting the fear that lurked inside the pompous old man's eyes. "That I did, and the only way that spell can be undone will be when my immortality comes to greet me."

Magnus seemed confused. He eyed Isra carefully, knowing that such spells from a mighty witch as she was could only be undone when death came forth ... but wasn't she impenetrable from death?

This cannot ever be, he thought, hoping the witch wasn't able to translate his thoughts. "But you are immortal, are you not?" he questioned.

She smiled, glancing across the rueful bodies that were present today: the wise owl she had always found to be inspiring, Otto, and then Lady Vama and the courageous young man whom she did not yet know his name that had her senses entranced with wonder. She kept her attention focused on the dark blonde individual for a moment, giving him her watchful eye before turning back to Magnus.

"I am immortal. That is known. You must remember everything conspires throughout time so even I, a spirit that possesses great magic, will at some point in time have a date with perilous destiny," she muttered with a smile.

Otto Jinx looked over at Magnus, signaling him to stop with one coarse stare. Magnus looked across to Otto Jinx, acknowledging him magnanimously. Magnus then looked at Isra. Isra stared at Magnus. The young gentleman looked over at both Magnus and Isra, curious to know what was commencing between them. The young man viewed Isra as bold and brash while Magnus appeared to be old and stuffy, although he proclaimed to be wise and renowned for his laws of magic.

Isra laughed again in an attempt to defuse the silence. "My, what a sore selection of fruits this is! Reprimanding me for enchanting my lover! Are the council's ways so dull and boring they feel the need to impose them onto everyone else? My goodness, there must be worse crimes! You know I don't abide by your lightly ways!" she retorted sternly, remembering Astrid was in the room in his raven form.

Magnus replied coldly, "The council does not approve of this man! We believe the two of you are far too dangerous to exist together. Both with potent minds. Revolting hearts entwined. It's just too cataclysmic. The things you could accomplish, well it doesn't bear moral thought. Never mind the ill-fated peril that you call love."

Astrid went extra quiet. Staying out of sight, focusing on the choice words. He and Isra had never done magic together. He didn't pursue dark magic as much as she, but he did, when it suited him. He just wasn't too keen over the council deciding his union with Isra was wrong. Surely, he and Isra would be the judge of that?

"Then there's the matter of the girl" Magnus added.

Astrid went quiet from his perch. He knew what was coming next.

The girl? Isra thought intriguingly, putting her fingers to her lips as she gasped in mid thought. "Oh, our dear beloved Contessia!" she announced with a high-pitched squeal.

"Yes. The Wiccan girl you took from her home and subdued into darkness," he said as he noted Isra's choice to keep Contessia under lock and key by owning her mortal soul.

"Oh. I had forgotten about her for a moment there."

Magnus started again, noticing Isra's amusement. "Yes, well your lover has been, shall we say, toying with her?"

Isra smiled. "Why yes, Astrid has been toying with the fragile girl's mind. I would scold him but you know men of his nature. She was a toy to his illicit boredom and nothing more."

"Toying with someone is one thing; mentally tormenting somebody so they believe they are lost in their own mind is another altogether!"

Isra laughed him off unapologetically. "Oh nonsense! Be gone with your lurid mockery! If the girl was in charge of her emotions, and I know Contessia isn't, Astrid wouldn't have toyed with her in the first place! You cannot blame my companion when the girl is unstable," she finished coldly.

She eyed the onlookers for a moment, unrelenting. "But the girl is well treated here. She is part of the furniture. I even find myself growing on her."

Isra thought back to Astrid's treatment of Contessia. She had known what he was up to, she had just kept quiet about it. Astrid had tormented Contessia in the most horrid way. On her first evening in the tower, Astrid put her through a hellish nightmare, sending her into a dark mysterious tunnel that had lured poor Contessia into quite a fright. Beyond the door that had been magickally conjured lurked a horrifying row of spiders.

Isra had no clue why Astrid had done it to Contessia, but she knew he must have had his reasons although he was a peculiar soul and would do things rashly without good cause as she often did.

Never mind, it's not important, Isra reminded herself before going into another tangent of thought. Astrid would do his dark deeds and she would do hers. Isra knew Astrid had a dark side but she knew better than anyone that everyone has a dark side, even if it's not seen right away. It would soon greet you when you least expected it.

"Unstable she may be, yes, but she was a perfect victim at the hands of your lover so affectionately named Sir Astrid," Magnus chided through another sip of delectable orange tea before pursing his lips and starting again. "We believe this union is far too dangerous to exist."

Astrid was careful not to make a sound now. Anxious and angry, but still he kept his cool. *So, I'm a sir now,* he thought to himself sarcastically. *I never realized I had gone up in the world since being entangled with a witch,* he mused as he continued to listen, the noise of the droning voices starting to wear down on the tower walls.

Isra chided sarcastically, "If that is the way of it, I may just ask him to marry me! Let's see how your dreary reasoning feels about that."

Magnus looked at Isra crossly. "This is no time for amusement, Lady Isra."

Isra chuckled, her voice lowering as she spoke. "A dangerous man you perceive him to be, but I am the creator of his current form and it is only I that will scold him if such an event ever arises." Isra got up from her chair, proceeding to move toward the door.

Magnus did not look satisfied as he too got up from his seat at the table. "And that is your final word?"

Isra held the door open impatiently for Magus, subtly telling him she wanted him to go. She caught sight of Astrid on the shelf. Smiling, she waved a finger at him, encouraging him to join her.

"You have expressed your concerns. I will be sure to send you an invitation to the wedding!" she joked, sarcasm running amok in her voice.

Magnus looked astonished. "I see. Well, I bid you good day, Lady Isra. I hope we never meet again," he said, resentment echoing through his manner as he spoke.

Lady Isra led him down the long staircase that descended to the main ornate door. Astrid flew beside her, staying within safe proximity of Isra and Magnus. Lady Isra opened the door, looking like she might hurl Magnus straight through it, but instead she maintained her composure, holding the door ajar and gesturing him to exit. Otto Jinx and Lady Vama came down the stairs, both glancing at and acknowledging Lady Isra fondly.

Otto flew down, carefully landing on the bottom of the staircase as he looked up toward Isra and voiced, "I wish today could have been a more pleasant occasion, but oh well, good to see you nonetheless, Isra! I hope that the universe treats you well."

Isra smiled as she held out her hand for her former teacher, allowing him to rest on her arm. "I hope so too, dear Sir. I imagine we will meet again," she said fondly, gazing at him, her eyes edging around his brown textured feathers before the owl tenderly flew away, following Magnus Wingdom out of the door.

The dark blonde figure approached nervously, extending his hand. "Good day, Lady Isra. I am Ronald. I wish to become a warlock," he announced.

Lady Isra studied the young man carefully. She smelled a musky odor symbolizing vigor and passion. He appeared robust yet slender in his form.

"Well young man, I am afraid your introduction hasn't been at the most pleasant of occasions, but naturally I am pleased to make your acquaintance," she expressed with curiosity.

"Perhaps we could meet again?" Ronald posed.

"Perhaps. In the meantime, I have some business to attend to."

Astrid softly landed on the witch's shoulder, nudging her affectionately behind her ear. Isra smiled as the raven settled comfortably on her, swiftly turning her focus onto Ronald. "Oh, how rude of me!" she exclaimed. "This is Astrid, the man of the house."

The mortal Ronald and Astrid gave each other wide-eyed, curious stares as both male counterparts gave each other a thorough going-over. Feeling both cautious and nervous as both engaged in this intriguing meeting of the minds, Ronald's eyes couldn't handle the pressure of Astrid's forceful, cold stare, and his gaze fell to the floor as the raven looked triumphant. Astrid's eyes remained on Ronald as the intimidated mortal returned his focus back to Lady Isra.

"Well, it has been a pleasure, I must say. I bid you good day." He then made his way out of the main door.

Lady Isra felt relief as she shut the oak door behind Ronald. He was the last of them. All of the unwanted guests had made their exit, much to her content and amusement. She turned to the raven with much furor, her eyes glancing upon his soft feathers as she placed a kiss upon his head. Her lips delicately pressed upon him as she carefully demonstrated her treasured regard for the bold, black creature.

"Finally," she voiced.

"Peace at last," he announced in recognition, turning his head to her face. "But I think I'd prefer to touch you in the way I am more partial toward."

The witch smiled, saying nothing.

In a flash, just like lightning, the black feathers were gone, elegantly replaced with smooth, dark hair and generous arms that beautifully wrapped themselves around her neck as strong fingers entwined with her, pressed warmly in a flutter of love and rapid expression.

"Kiss me," he beamed, looking at her slowly, his eyes glowing at hers.

"I thought you'd never ask," she whispered, allowing Astrid into her mouth as he showed her just how much he had missed her.

6

The dusk air was coming through the window. The black carpet of night was becoming more prominent as the sun disappeared from view. Astrid turned to Isra, changing his focus from excited to serious without blinking.

"We need to talk about things," he said eagerly.

He stopped for a moment. The pain began to emerge in his head. He felt it in his humanized body, running all the way down to his bones. He looked at her softly as if he was about to burst into tears.

"I mean, about when you died."

Her eyes fell upon him in a blaze of silence. Her head tilted toward his as it leaned against his strong chest. The deafening silence around them grew bolder as she made no sound. She pressed against him, feeling the softness of his skin. Her hands were positioned by his chest as she felt the beat of his tender, fragile heart. Her untimely death undoubtedly brought much pain and suffering that vibrated deep into the raven-man's warm heart.

"I don't remember it," she disclosed. Her face focused on him as she tried to recall what it was like to die.

He pulled her away from his heart, looking at her. "I do," he admitted. A tear gently left the duct inside his eye. "You can never know how much you need someone until they are no longer beside you."

He tried his utmost to remain calm as he recalled the painful event. "I thought you were gone forever, lost in the sands of time as I sat on that grassy bank inconsolable."

He kept his composure, his eyes fixed upon her. His mind drifted back to him in his raven form, devastated that his love had left him in such a fast and unexpected way on that fateful day. He closed his eyes and continued.

"You think you understand pain. The pain you feel right now is nothing compared to the dazzling rush that courses inside your blood as it turns cold as ice, lost without its fire. No longer being able to set your eyes on your faithful human companion, the pain you feel is a rush that comes upon you swiftly and all you can do is accept it as you try aimlessly to mend your broken soul, feeling the cracks that encircle your entire being as you go into repair. After a time, the pain fades, but it never goes away. You're unborn and unbroken after blood has spilled, but the cycle begins again with the calling of spring and thus, new life begins."

Isra turned to him, trying to perceive his pain as she was not able to remember a single segment of it. She tried to be comforting. "I never imagined death that way," she lamented.

"Worse was when the rain came and the snow disintegrated into the white, murky liquid, nonexistent in a dreary, grime-filled reality leaving nothing behind but the fierce stain of blood."

His mind feeling unsettled returned to the day that rapidly turned into a cloudy night, the rain pelting hard as it fell onto the ground. Rain splattered all over Lady Isra's fragile body as it fell into a pool around her. The blood refused to fade as it lingered around her perfect form poetically.

Astrid, unable to accept her death and consumed with devastation, enchanted himself back into his raven form, hating every aspect of his human self, no longer wanting a reminder of everything that he had lost. He was gloomy, desolate. His loss reactivated all the pain he had ever known.

Later as the evening breeze descended across the land, ravens from all over gathered around the witch and Astrid, looking upon her and her lover as he resided by her side, refusing to be anywhere else. The rain still pelted her body as Astrid watched the moon emerge between the trees, showing a glimmer of hope as it rose in the sky.

It was then that Astrid saw more than just a wave of hope. He saw a climatic spark of lightning shake the world with a mighty force as it thundered boldly, colliding with the skies. The white sparks of light surrounded the witch as they formed a protective bubble, encapsulating her inside its wide and bright velocity. The penetrative act of force diligently engaged around the witch, illuminating her body.

Fascinated, Astrid's tears faded away, his sight sharply pressed on the majestic design that was occurring right in front of him. Lady Isra was glowing with a radiant spectrum of white light, brighter than anything Astrid had seen before. He twitched as he was sure he saw her chest rise.

No, it can't be, he thought. *She's dead.* He figured it was just his imagination, caused by his bewilderment and grief. But Astrid looked closer and sure enough, Isra's chest rose again. He was astounded at the miracle that was happening as a ghostly figure emerged.

Astrid watched keenly as the figure approached the witch's body, bending down upon her. Astrid thought the figure may have wanted to kiss her because of how he was positioned; he presumed it was male by the nature of it.

A cloudy wave of smoke appeared as the figure revealed itself. The head of a snake gazed at Astrid as he stared in disbelief. The green eyes that protruded from inside the head reverently stared back at him. He remembered those eyes. It was Romeo, Isra's friend and confidant. The raven and the snake exchanged glances.

Astrid was puzzled at Romeo's appearance but then he saw the snake had no body, just a spirit form. Romeo was truly dead but here he was, somehow bringing Lady Isra back to life.

Romeo turned to face the raven. "Do not be alarmed. I am very much in my immortality, but she is not. Not now."

Astrid rose silently, reaching for Isra as he saw her eyes flicker in the light of the moon. Romeo's spirit mumbled something silently to her as Astrid looked on.

"I'm not alarmed. What are you doing here?" Astrid probed.

"I heard the avalanche from the murkiest depths of my perishment. I had to come to her," Romeo professed as Astrid stared at him wildly.

"Yes, but why? You betrayed her! Why would you save her?" Astrid prodded.

Romeo's head lifted as he addressed Astrid. "Because despite my transgression that led to my ill-fated death, I *had* to come and save her. It was the only way I could make up for my misdeed."

Astrid's feathers ruffled as the nightly winds riled through him. "No. I can't find any reason why you would save her unless it was a guilty conscience you had serving you!" He noted the look of remorseful loss resounding upon Romeo's face. "Why were you killed? At least tell me that?" Astrid questioned.

"It was due to an enemy, an unsightly presence filled with rage and power. Isra's foe," Romeo announced calmly.

His spirited form was clearly sending the raven abuzz with questions and rightly so. He thought he had just lost his love forever. Astrid paused. Isra had a lot of foes. He had to narrow it down. He looked at Romeo in a way that said, "Tell me more" without actually saying the words. He stared into Romeo's eyes. That wise old soul that had made itself known to Isra on the very first day they had made their acquaintance was making him fathom every single element inside his being.

"There was one. A fair-haired maiden from Isra's deeply hidden past when she was a light being. She told me that she and Isra parted ways over an unrequited love."

Unrequited love? That struck Astrid's tongue like a sour lemon. He didn't know all of Isra's past, but he had known that she had been the victim of a deeply painful love, one that was not reciprocated. He continued to think as he processed all of the information together. Fair haired. Deeply hidden past.

Oh my, it could only have been one...

Astrid glanced up at Romeo, eying the snake spirit seriously as he asked, "You don't mean Everilda do you?"

Romeo smiled, acknowledging Astrid before replacing his focus back onto the witch. "The one who was killed moments before Isra. It was the indefinable witch's death that caused the avalanche! It sent a ripple throughout the cosmos and nature responded."

"So Everilda killed you!" Astrid insinuated.

"That is correct," Romeo concurred.

Astrid's gaze bounced back and forth all over the reptilian spirit as he studied the creature's form cautiously. So much was surmising all around him at this moment as he allowed these revelations to sink in. Everilda had killed Romeo! Everilda had sought out Isra as her target long before she had made herself known. It was all part of a much grander plan!

The bleakness of night shone as the moon showed its valor brightly. Astrid looked up from his train of thought, only to find Romeo had gone, vanished. Astrid glanced at himself and then Isra. In a moment of clarity, he was back in his human form again.

He ambled toward where Isra lay, swooping down and picking her up in his arms. Her body as light as a cloud, he held her. Smiling, he looked beneath him, softly lifting her toward him as he lowered his lips to her own, aware that they were soaking wet from the rain, dripping with moist pleasure as he felt the rough texture they embedded. Closing his eyes, he planted a kiss on her rain-splattered lips, not that she would feel it in her state of sedation.

As the rain continued to plummet down, Astrid looked ahead. The tower was in sight, just a short distance away, but he'd have to transport Isra there in his arms since she would not awaken for a while. She would have no memory of any of this.

The shadows beckoned and Astrid realized he was in the tower with Isra. She sat beside him and listened as he told her the story of her resurrection. She was in awe of him, his words gripping and holding her. He had never seen her so perfectly still and yet here she was, eyes on him, lips pursed in anticipation of more.

"I have never known a night to be as memorable as that one," he commented.

Isra stopped for a moment. Her thoughts began to ferment inside of her, and if she wasn't careful, she thought her head might explode with wonder and curiosity. "But what about Romeo? Did he say goodbye?" she queried.

"No. He didn't. He was gone in a flash. One moment I was thinking, the next he was nowhere to be seen."

Isra paused again, looking at Astrid for signs of something that could be found in his lingering voice. Having closure on Romeo was something she had been seeking for a long time. He was a friend she held in very high esteem and then one day he had been vanquished, stabbed so ferociously that the green slime that resembled his reptilian blood plundered forever down that ancient oak tree.

Astrid looked at Isra with much serious thought. "But when I arrived back here with you in my arms, I found that many things had occurred as a result of your death."

He drew back into his mind as he recalled the black cloud that lingered above the tower as he approached it on that rainy night. It stood out like a silhouette, black and full of foreboding. Who knew that the death of a witch could cause such a tremendous ripple effect? As he entered through the ornate, antique door carrying Isra in his arms, he noticed that not only was the building deserted, but an air of intense fear haunted the walls.

A sound could be heard from the basement. It seemed like muffled voices.

Astrid had laid Isra on the couch, watching her hair fall to one side of her face as she slept ever so peacefully before he ran down to discover what the noise was. The basement was as grim as ever. Dark and dank. Contessia was down on the floor, weeping. Her entire body shook with climatic fear.

Astrid then noticed Klinq crouched in the corner, refusing to look at Contessia, but both of them were filled with such hatred for one another. It was clearly observed as the raven-man watched them both with backs turned and eyes narrowed at the sight of the other participant.

Astrid turned to Contessia. "What happened here?"

Contessia mused as she looked at Astrid; here was a man who had inflicted great torture upon her, making her hate her very soul while he reveled in her distress. She was terrified at the sight of him. Just those dark eyes made her blood turn. She could feel it pulsing away, getting hotter as he glanced at her. It was intoxicating. It was as though her blood was boiling inside her with just one look from the raven-man.

"I don't remember!" she gasped, doing her best to not make eye contact. She was feeling incredibly nauseous at the sight of Astrid.

Astrid looked over to Klinq in his corner, striding up to the gnome as he dragged him up from the floor. "And you, what the hell are you doing here?"

Klinq tried to remain calm as Astrid held him forcefully in his grip. "You dragged me down here, remember?"

Astrid did remember. There was quite a showdown between Klinq and Contessia. Klinq was as terrified then as he was now, but now he was also angry. The anger seemed to have given the gnome some balls.

Astrid mocked the gnome as he managed a false smile teamed with folded arms and a cross exterior. "Ah, yes, I do. You have no place among this kind! In the name of Lady Isra, I banish you, Sir Klinq, from the land, never to return; for if you do, there will be dire consequences."

Klinq said nothing. His face was desolate and full of fear as the strong and bold raven-man spoke before him.

"And now go," Astrid instructed, pointing to the door on the left.

Astrid looked as if he were about to drag Klinq out of the tower and there was a good chance he would, so Klinq stood up weakly and ran, leaving behind his favorite wooly hat as he leaped away swiftly. He realized the hat was missing but carried on running as he placed his hands on his head aimlessly in his flight.

Contessia looked slightly flushed as she watched the interaction between Astrid and Klinq from her safe distance, albeit only a foot away, but it was safe enough in her mind to know that Klinq was going away. Sadly, the Wiccan girl was under a spell, but nothing but hatred in her heart remained for the dull, dimwitted gnome now. Contessia felt at peace now that Klinq would no longer be present in the vicinity.

Astrid grimaced at Contessia, disgusted with her in many ways as he sternly approached her. "You will remain here until such time when I say otherwise. You are not to leave this room. Do you hear me?" he barked.

Contessia, full of fear, simply nodded. Astrid turned away, venturing out of the room. The sound of paper rustling could be heard and Astrid looked up to see Isra sitting opposite him.

"So, you banished Klinq from the lands!"

"Yes," he said softly. "After your death, I felt it was in your best interests to have him gone. I told that horrid girl she was to remain in that basement for all eternity until I let her know otherwise that it was okay for her to be free. I didn't want anyone knowing what had happened to you."

He breathed softly, a small tear exiting his eye and crawling down his cheek as he expressed the emotion. "And with both of them out of the way, I could concentrate on your recovery. It wasn't easy. I doubt you'd remember the first few days. You were so weak and weary, but I also needed to know if you were still immortal, if something of great magnitude could happen again. That's why as soon as you were somewhat rested, I went away."

He hesitated to continue, noting Isra was being quieter than her usual self. The tale of her death combined with her supernatural resurrection were clearly having a very significant effect on the witch, something Astrid could not have predicted as she was always confident and cool in the face of any serious situation. In this instance, she was not. Her face was pale, her lips the shade of burning blood. Her eyes glinted like facets of emeralds dipped in fire.

Astrid was right: Isra wasn't able to recollect much. She remembered the stain on her dress, a vile maroon color as the tears in the bright white material reminded her just how close she'd come to no longer being present on this plane of existence.

She had remembered Astrid being present by her side. He was always there when she was drifting in and out of sleep as she did in those gentle moments where her body was too fragile to withstand any amount of activity, and so she ceased to do anything except slumber.

"When you were strong enough and your eyes stayed open for longer than a few hours, I made the decisive move to undertake further investigation into your condition. I had to make sure that if something like this or an even dire cause of harm was made, you would without a doubt survive."

Isra was surrounded by questions. Questions she had so far not asked but had wanted to for an insurmountable period of time. She gazed upon the handsome raven-man with such admiration and design that it could not be faltered from her mind. "The freezing spell still captured them despite my death?"

"Yes. But you didn't cast it," Astrid calmly answered, his dark brown eyes emitting gold flecks as he stared at her, knowing that he was right. "I don't know who did, but I know it wasn't you."

Isra stopped, her mouth open at Astrid having possession of this knowledge, but before she could utter a word, her attention was caught by something tapping loudly on the window. The sound pulsated in her ear drums as it grew more prominent.

7

———————

Astrid watched Isra go over to the window. Her hands grazed across the ebony window frame as she grasped the handle, pressing it downward as she pushed the glass structure open. To her surprise and Astrid's, a large black raven flew in through the window, landing swiftly on her arm.

Astrid glowered, feeling jealous that another black feathered creature was making acquaintance with his love. Something about this raven seemed familiar. He scratched his head, not knowing what it was, but it pulsated through his body as Isra looked toward the magnificent being.

The raven swallowed gently, looking up at her with much respect as it bowed its head before its beak opened and words came out. "I am sorry. I do not mean to intrude. I have been searching for you for such a long time!"

Isra was perplexed by such a statement but stood openly and allowed the raven to speak.

The raven looked at Isra, acknowledging her patience as he babbled on. "I am Silas. I am from a land quite some distance from here. Spirisity. Have you heard of it?"

Astrid's face dropped at once. He knew just who this raven was.

He couldn't quite believe it. He was astonished that such a thing could be conceivable, but his eyes were open; he wasn't losing his mind and it was occurring right in his domain.

Astrid courageously turned to face Silas. His eyes were almost glaring and yet also smiling at the majestic creature. His arms folded, he moved forward fearlessly. "It took you a long time, brother!"

Silas turned his head around. "Brother? Oh goodness! Astrid, it can't be you! But what happened to your feathers?"

He seemed comical as he said it. Silas was always one for jokes. He loved a good worm on a hot, sunny day but he also loved a jolly laugh. He couldn't understand why his brother was covered in this peach textured matter, even though he recognized the dark hazel eyes immediately.

"And what are those stumpy tall things that seem to have impetuously replaced your claws?" he questioned.

Astrid smiled as his brother flew over, gaining a keen view of him as he landed on Astrid's shoulder. "I'm human now," he confessed.

"Well, it does explain that unorthodox coloring that you proudly own. It looks good on you as a matter of fact!" Silas mused, collectively focused on Astrid's tall and slender body that made him feel as if he were looking upon a giant and not his flesh and blood that had transformed from a bird to a man.

Silas laughed quietly as he looked at Astrid's ruffled, messy hair. "I think I'll keep my feathers."

Isra noticed this notion and laughed cheerily, her face resounding a shade of blossom pink as she felt the amusement from Silas. She wondered if Astrid missed his feathers. Did he miss his life as a raven? Maybe he was missing some part of his physical aspects as a bird, but he seemed complacent enough in his contentment with her, so she let the thought pass.

Isra turned to both males and smiled. "I think I will leave you two fine fellows to this private and delicate matter." She softly swept over to Astrid, placing a kiss on his cheek before she promptly left the scene.

Astrid mused, as he watched Isra's long flowing gown disappear after her, watching her elegant flow as she strode away. He calmly took a breath as he began. "I fell in love with Isra shortly after we met. Later, she created the human body I reside in."

His face dropped slightly as he didn't know how Silas would react. His brother had never really approved of the decisions Astrid made in his life. He wasn't sure how Silas would react to him being in union with a witch.

Hang on, he thought, *why are you seeking Isra? You said you had been searching for her for a long time!*

This thought perplexed him. He was bemused. Why would his brother be searching for his one true love? He couldn't figure it out. He thought he was the only raven who'd fallen in love with her bewitching heart. He was the one who found himself engrossed in her energy-filled mind. He couldn't imagine anyone else coming to take his place.

This is fucking crazy, he thought. *I should just ask him what he is doing here. I have no reason to be jealous! So why the hell am I? It's ludicrous!*

He didn't stop his heart racing as he allowed the torturing thought to squeal silently inside as he struggled to utter words. His mouth opened to express a sound. He didn't want to sound presumptuous or stupid. Neither was among his fine array of qualities.

He wanted to be seen as a man. A strong man who had his life together and could handle anything! He didn't want to be weak, like a hatchling that had no prime knowledge of the treacherous world they had been born into. Astrid contemplated the thought as he postulated his voice clearly. Gawking at Silas, one eye turned to his left side, he began to express it.

"Silas please don't see me as out of line as I say this, but why are you here in Isra's kingdom?"

Astrid in his insecure manner found himself gaping at Silas as the raven made no effort to pick at the question that was thrown his way. Instead, he grasped the concept that his now human brother was insecure despite this intense and passionate relationship with a witch, a witch that was very much buried in the ways of the occult and the unknown. She wasn't a stranger to the dark and sometimes the light merged with her, and both could be united in a happy conclusion, but primarily she was dark, hidden, and more so, she knew it.

Astrid however was more reserved than Isra. Silas had long observed Astrid's behaviors since they were small, minute hatchlings and he knew Astrid didn't have the best of luck when it came to love. There was no doubt that the love with Isra was true, but as Silas perused deep into his brother's soul, he could see the raven-man was very unsure of Isra's feelings for him, part of him wondering if she would leave him, a feeling that made him feel complacent and lost within himself.

If Silas spent enough time delving into his brother's complex mind, he would be able to see all of the facets. The anxiety and fear that hounded him as a result of his previous lovers left him with nothing but a pitted broken heart that was worn from too many battles.

Most of this Silas had clear knowledge of. In the romance area, Astrid didn't flourish as much as the other males. It was hard for him to find a mate and so after a time of lonesomeness and falling for the wrong females, he became solitary, living life by the side of the full moon and singing sweetly, gobbling up delicious, tasty worm morsels as he cawed after something desirable.

It was a life that had fulfillment, intrigue, and wonder. Astrid wanted it, a life he had always wanted for himself: to be happy and cared for by another while being able to give his own sweet love to a dearly beloved companion, a companion he could share everything with and feel content and at peace with himself within the connection. Silas paused. Something outside had distracted him, but he paid it no mind and returned his focus to Astrid.

He could only speak the truth to Astrid and so Silas breathed out a heavy sigh as he cleared his throat. "I'm here because your Lady Isra is in great danger."

Astrid took great heed of the news at once. His heart beat inside his chest as if it was going to burst at any minute. He clutched his chest while trying his utmost to remain calm. Who was he fooling? He had already lost Isra once. He most certainly did not want it to happen again. He would implicitly give up his own life before seeing her die in his arms again.

He walked over to the old-fashioned pot that lay by the window frame to gather fresh coffee beans and his thoughts. He placed the beans in an empty cup and allowed the water to filtrate as it came to a bubbling boil. After a few moments, he retrieved the pot, carefully pouring the hot water over the fresh beans. The infusion came to a blistering whirl as it swirled around like a vortex inside the cup. He stared blankly at the ceiling as he brought the tantalizing brew of steam forward, allowing small sips of the fragrant beverage to linger inside his mouth.

Astrid slammed the cup down on the bay by the window, causing the astringent brown liquid to cascade all over the clear glass. His hands fell to his sides, shaking with penetrative force. Standing beside the window, he drew back his energy, taking a breath as he tried to regain his focus.

He was reaching into the unknown with his repented vision or so it seemed as he placed his attention on the floor, his eyes slowly traveling back up to face Silas. "How is she in danger? Why is she in danger?"

Silas flew over and landed on the window ledge, being careful not to step into the mess left by the caffeinated beverage. He cleared his throat before moving closer to Astrid's position. "You might want to get into a seated position," Silas warned, feeling the climatic waves of anxiety vibrating from Astrid.

Astrid glared at Silas, maintaining his standing arrangement and holding a manly stance as he rested his hands on the windowsill, refusing to sit. "I don't want to fucking seat myself anywhere or anyplace! Just tell me, will she succumb to immortality again?" Astrid pleaded, showing a vulnerability that glowed from inside him.

"Yes. She may succumb to immortality. A mortal holds her responsible for the destruction of his family."

Astrid looked up with clarity, his eyes protruding as the thought echoed through his mind. "She destroyed the life of a mortal two years ago. She took everything he loved. Is it him? Is this the one that seeks revenge?"

Silas smiled. "The mortal being who seeks revenge is in many senses a warlock. Alas, he does not yet possess the power he wishes, so he must learn his craft, focus his strengths, and learn his weaknesses in order to succeed."

"It is not who I thought," Astrid concurred.

He began to think. His mind whizzed around as he pedaled through the congregating thoughts revolving in his head. Astrid dug deep into his memoires, tugging away at the fabrications and the complex synchronistic energy that plagued his head. The noise in him, pulsating inside, added pressure to his already foreboding mind. The throbbing added rhythm as he focused on the premise.

Who was seeking revenge against his Isra? Who would be pedantically so determined to find his witch, maneuvering their unique expertise in training to find her?

He couldn't figure it out. Everilda was dead, so it wasn't her. There was no family left of Kane to speak of, so that was also unlikely. Anyone else she had ever encountered was banished to perishable lengths in the darkest voids of Hell.

Astrid had gone on a blank, his memory failing him in his mission. Silas had given him very small, segmented pieces, but the rest of the puzzle lacked clarity. If the final piece was going to fit, it would need to show constructive lucidity, showing Astrid the perpetrator's identity.

"No. The individual that you fathomed it to be, it's not them. They don't possess the magnitude needed to conquer your Isra."

Astrid breathed a sigh of relief; he could relax knowing it wasn't Kane. But the puzzle was still incomplete...

8

Isra looked ahead as she studied the sunshine flowers gracing the meadow below her feet and smelling every one as she admired their beauty.

The crimson red apples looked delectable as they hung on their respective tempting branches. The apple tree stood out in a mass of flowers and floral fancy on its own. A shadow appeared beside Isra startling her as it grew bolder with its energetic frequency. She turned to face the shadow, only to find a purple mass emerging beneath a shadowed black cloak.

"Oh, it's you, child!" Isra uttered.

Contessia was standing over her.

"Sorry, sister. I grew tired of the lack of fresh air," Contessia murmured as she stood close to Isra, feeling the cool spring breeze on her face.

"No. It's no quandary. I knew you'd come out of your solitude sooner or later," Isra said warmly. "You just startled me a little is all. Astrid has pleasant company so I made myself scarce so they could converse in peace."

Isra made herself comfortable in the dewy grass, lowering herself down into the green softness. Contessia swallowed a little at the thought of Astrid. The raven-man still gave her chills as she remembered his torture of her.

He had acted with the most ferocious malice toward her. She had not done anything to incur his wrath to warrant such acts of cruelty, but she had been his plaything and he had conspicuously subjected her to the foulest aspects of his underworld.

"Ah. I tend not to get involved in any elements pertaining to your companion," Contessia admitted.

She lowered her form to the bottom of nature's well as she joined her sister Isra on the grass. Her purple hair blew casually in the wind, covering her face as she settled herself cozily upon the luscious green blanket.

"I can still sometimes feel spiders climbing up my back, but then I wake up and remember that it's just an illusion. A terrifying relentless phantasm haunts me at every turn," she uttered quietly with a shiver.

"I know," Isra acknowledged as she saw the fear in Contessia's bold eyes, carefully remembering the torture her lover had exacted upon the girl and feeling guilty because she had almost exacted the same. She had much compassion for Contessia now, understanding the horror and pain that lurked within her, pain and horror that Isra had once felt although she would never lay claim to it in words. "I hope that time is passed between us now."

Contessia almost smiled, her fear subsiding as she felt the warmth that had grown between her and Isra in such a short space of time. Like flames to fire, the two women had an understanding of how tidings were, more so they accepted it and carried on fearlessly despite the adversity.

"I still don't know why he did such things to me!" Contessia pondered.

"I am afraid I am none the wiser. I would scold him, but alas, my heart is entwined with his. He has always been loyal to me in life and death," Isra remarked with much ambiguity.

"It is no quarrel," Contessia proclaimed. "It still would have been nice to have an apology for his merciless actions."

Isra went quiet. Her heart sank. She had known behavior from men to be without mercy long before Contessia had even been formed in the womb. She had remembered the horrific ways in which her heart had been furiously torn open, showing the most vulnerable parts of herself time and time again as yet another man consumed the most fragile of hearts: hers. Isra understood the pain of never being told why they had exacted such poison toward her. More importantly, she had grandstanded the pain more times than she had cared to know.

"Unfortunately, child, the world can be cruel and without comfort. This I know," she finished gravely.

Contessia lifted her head, understanding her sister's corroboratory story. "That gives meaning to what your foe did to me. I think I can recall her name. Edith. Edie?"

"Everilda," Isra confirmed. "Her name was Everilda. The guise she befouled you with was a false one."

"Alas, I did not have knowledge of it at the time," Contessia admitted. She felt stupid at not seeing through the mortal's facade.

"Everilda was an individual filled with rage and power or hopes of attaining such power. She was a failure. Jealous. Bitter with no comprehension for another soul except herself. She was fixated on her ego and that immaculately led to her defeat because she was so obsessed with obtaining all she felt she deserved, she failed to notice her weakness and that was what led to her untimely end," Isra told Contessia.

Contessia was curious as she pursed her lips. "How did you defeat her?" she asked before she could stop herself with her own reason. She felt like her curiosity got her into more woe than she could anticipate but for some reason, she still pursued her voyage head on.

Isra became silent, gently aroused in her triumph as she recalled the clever means in which she had taken Everilda down. Excited, she finally voiced, "I did it by using the one thing Everilda had never experienced in her life."

Contessia was perplexed. She couldn't understand what Isra was referring to. "And what was that?" she probed.

"Love. Something so fragile and yet so rare. Everilda had never possessed such a beautiful fragment of emotion, thus giving me the power to end her dynasty with one simple flash of lightning," Isra attested.

Isra began with a tinge in her cheeks, the emotion thrilling her as she recalled her tale. "It was a dark night, the skies showing a shade of cobalt blue with lingering tufts of black creeping out from behind the clouds. I stood on the grassy spot, the cool night air wafting over me, mumbling the right words to summon my enemy. The apparition was just after, and Everilda appeared in a flash. I remember the red. Red surrounded her in a twist of the most felonious lightning I have ever known. Everilda wasn't best pleased at being called to her position. We exchanged bittersweet words reminding me of our earlier days. She was misty with her lack of wit and the ability to form a solid sentence, but I had something she didn't."

Isra paused as she recalled the night in which the red embers burned so deeply in her heart. The fire in her was unmistakable. The love that she carried from Astrid burned so brightly nothing could dull its pungent flavor. It was a force beyond anything she had mustered. Nothing could break this love. Not power, not force. Nothing.

"The fire that inspired me was surging through me like a malevolent wave that night. I just kept focusing on Astrid. Our combined energy that we share every time we connect, and the power was more than I could imagine! It was wrenching me through me, I could feel it coursing through every inch of my soul," Isra declared.

Contessia hung onto every word, deeply enthralled and entertained by Isra's story. Her eyes locked onto Isra's in a connective focus and her hand slowly moved away from her mouth as she tried to contain the fear and excitement from within.

Isra saw the child's enthused demeanor and carried on with a subtle smile. It brought her joy, knowing she could bring wisdom and regaling words to another.

"It was the visual imagery that did the most futile damage. I saw Everilda weakening as I opened my eyes, but still connected to that indescribable energy that was surging across the whole of the area where we stood."

The pause in which Isra broke her flow for just a moment sent a penetrative silence, one that Contessia felt come upon her in waves. The next few minutes consisted of the two women sitting, exchanging nothing but looks as Contessia longed to hear the rest. Isra took a small breath in. She remembered the moment well. One word was all it took to destroy Everilda. The cataclysm was followed by a rupture in the eons as the word Isra uttered caused ripples across the universe to come flying in at all directions. Everilda was to be delivered her final reward.

"It was the word I spoke that set everything ablaze. Love. Who knew that one tiny word I believed to be so low and deprecating in meaning for so many of my adult years could hold so much power? And the entire universe heard me. The sky was alive with the blood red sparks that electrified the entire scene in front of me. Everilda was surrounded as the mighty forces compassed her and reduced her to a pile of red dust that lay dormant on the forest floor," Isra finished as Contessia's eyes narrowed at the knowing of such a battle.

"Wow. I never imagined that you could do such good with your power!" Contessia exclaimed, almost shrieking as she tried to contain herself. This revelation was something that she had not prepared herself for and neither could she know how to.

"Well, it had been a very long time since these things have occurred," Isra explained as she carefully pulled her cloak closer to her, feeling a chill in her bones. "I feel weary, child. Perhaps we shall talk at greater lengths another time."

Contessia nodded, knowing that no words needed to be said. Her sister still felt some weakness from her recent "death." Contessia didn't know much about Isra's resurrection. She and Astrid kept it tightly wrapped and safe from listening ears, but she had overheard some conversations that she probably shouldn't have. Still, it wasn't her business to get involved.

Contessia watched as the blue shade of midnight fluctuated

through the ornate door, the cloak dragging on the floor as the door closed and Isra was no longer in sight.

~

ISRA SAT UPON HER COUCH, her legs outstretched as she sipped a warm apple tea.

Softly she gazed out of the window, admiring them all as she grasped within her consciousness the sights. Blossoming apple trees surrounded by sweet, pale pink roses that decorated the green grass in between the gold, sandy narrow path that joined the tower to the majestic grounds. Lavender flowers delicately framed the path; gracing both sides providing a warm contrast of yellow that diluted the boldness of the purple flora. The pretty, pastel view was serene to the restless witch as something on the shelf above her head grabbed her focus.

Looking up, she raised her eyes to the shelf to find them transfixed on a medium-sized jam jar dazzling at her in the brightest of turquoise colors. It was carefully labeled, "Do not open!"

Curious, Isra reached up and retrieved the jar, holding it in her hands as she examined the contents. The turquoise glimmered and shone effervescently back at her, then she noticed a tiny figure inside. Feeling a familiarity with the object inside, Isra looked closer.

Of course, she thought to herself and laughed.

It was Cora, the silly cottage girl Isra had enlisted to assist her in owning Contessia's soul in the battle against Everilda. Isra had forgotten about Cora since dying, but now the memory returned to her. The tiny girl looked cross as she banged helplessly against the jar, shrieking and wailing as the fierce spell that held her prisoner glowed violently, keeping her trapped inside the strong glass walls.

"Oh Cora, how I've missed you!" Isra cooed as she lifted the jar back onto the shelf. Smiling, Isra observed Cora's grimace with pleasant feeling. Wailing was heard again as Cora's jar was placed back in its home.

Isra ignored the girl's feeble cries as she heard footsteps behind her. Two hands were planted like silk, clinging on the top of her back just below her neck. Startled, she spun around as she was greeted with a smug smile with two sizzling brown eyes protrusive on her own.

"Astrid!" she squealed with a giggle as the raven-man lured her to him, pressing her to his chest and implanting her there with unyielding force as he kissed her sinfully, holding duress as he advanced inside her with powerful ardor.

"Sorry! I just couldn't help myself!" he joked with a twisted smile. "You looked so busy in your thought, so enthused in your task that I just had to pull your attention away with me! I know! I'm terrible. I should be put across your knee for a real good thrashing, but it might entertain me more to reverse our roles!" He grinned.

Isra felt her cheeks turn the bloodiest of reds. She blushed at the thought of Astrid placing her across his knee before exacting his nonviolent but yet sexy manner onto her. It felt entrancing. She blew the thought away from her mind as she smiled, imagining the heat between them if such a thing were brought into their reality.

"You'd like that, huh?" she posed flirtatiously.

"I would indeed," Astrid concurred.

Gently pulling himself away from Isra, his eyes fluttered abuzz as he seemed distracted. His eyes drifted to the same space as his mind as he found himself staring at the shelf that Isra had been focusing on when he had come in unexpectedly.

He then caught sight of the turquoise jar that stood out to him so vibrantly on the shelf. He admired the other items. Potion bottles, small vials of herbs, and various botanical items that Lady Isra had collected for use in magickal workings.

Intrigued, Astrid reached above Isra and picked up the blue jar, inspecting the contents as he did so. He didn't utter much surprise when he found it contained a tiny girl. He turned to Isra wickedly, a hint of mischief in his eye. Astrid laughed as the thought of it amused him.

"Is this what I think it is? You're putting people in jars now? How cute of you." A sweet taste of venom could be heard in his muttering as he continued to focus on the jar. "This is the girl who helped you with Contessia," Astrid perceived, the realization only just dawning on him.

How silly! he thought. *This jar had been lurking in the background the whole time and I never presumed it to be anything other than a tasteless decoration.*

"You don't have to say anything; I knew someone was assisting you, my love. I just didn't know who it was and since this charming thing is incarcerated in this miniature glass dungeon, I guess it was her!" he persisted, knowing he was at the source of truth.

Isra lowered her gaze as the raven-man cross examined her, eyeballing every part of her facial movements as if he was about to catch her out in some foul deception. He lifted her chin to his as he met her at eye level before kissing her lips again, softly expressing his devotion to her before he planted his lips on her tender earlobe, stroking it effortlessly with his tongue.

He closed his eyes as he whispered in her ear, the feel of his breath sending shivers down her neck as he did so. "I know you better than anyone. You're my twin soul! How silly of you to even try to hide something like this from me!"

Astrid opened his eyes to find them landing on a very nervous Isra. She clearly didn't enjoy his interrogation. She looked a little exposed. Shock emitted from her face as Astrid read that she was intimidated by his grueling furor of investigation. Her cheeks resembled a warm open fire with burnt coals. She was hot to the touch, boiling over with fear. Astrid had never seen Isra like this. He had never witnessed her scared, nor had he known her to possess an emotion as strong as fear.

Astrid lowered his voice, creating a ductile pleasure as he spoke. "I didn't mean that harshly," he began as his voice emitted tensions all across the room, vibrating between him and Isra. "But I had hoped in the duality of our connection there would be nothing you would hide from me."

Isra mouthed slowly, not knowing what to say. "I didn't mean to keep it from you, sweet Astrid, but Cora is a simple peasant, nothing more. She goaded me after our final business reached its conclusion. I snapped!" Isra confessed as Astrid looked over at her silently.

"I can see you snapped!"

He reached over and pulled Isra onto him, holding her there with firm agility as her face changed climates with her tone. Isra relented, backing down as Astrid held her robustly in his arms. He was durable in this form. He kept Isra firmly pressed onto him.

"You see, I was napping. I had this vision where a raven came to me, not you, dear one, but another. I woke up in a daze. Cora was looking down at me laughing. Her face was tinged with hilarity as she observed me waking from my semi-conscious dream."

Isra continued, her voice low. "And yet when I stood up, there she was still staring. Something inside me flipped. She was irritating me, so I locked her inside this glass jar! My deed is wicked, I know, but I felt provoked!"

Astrid scrutinized her form, looking her up and down as he worked his eyes across her. He felt compelled to look deeper into this. He knew Isra did horrid things. He knew inside this witch that he loved so dearly was a creature of vicious evil and death-defying power. But he was in love with that creature as well as the heart that he saw through when he had first laid eyes on her!

That beautiful moment where he had tapped on that cottage window, calling her name ... it resounded in his mind like a song but alas that was not the first time Astrid had caught sight of the witch. When he thought back to such a notion, he realized he had given himself away as he had known of her long before he had sought her out.

He remembered his words as he repeated them to himself silently in thought: *I know you do dark things, for it is in your nature to be dark.*

The truth of it was Astrid had been by Isra's side in her greatest hour of need, back when she was a teenager and she had been weeping over an unrequited love, although he never wanted to reveal such information to her for fear that she may strike against him, running away with the fear of her past.

But unbeknownst to Isra, Astrid had heard of her power from

other beings. He had led her to believe that he had wanted to assist her while also becoming her companion. Isra had no inclination that they would grow as close as they did, however it was Astrid's intention from the start that they would form a friendship and grow to love one another. That was always his most profound wish.

Now they were united in love and he was scared to tell her of the actual happenings in which he had come into her life. He feared greatly that if he divulged the memory of their past in which he had seen Isra, the light loving, sweet witch he had fallen for, she may see his keeping the truth from her as a betrayal.

The time for truth will indeed come, but not now! he thought.

"I know you do wicked things!" Astrid confirmed. "But it is in your nature to exact acts of torture, cruelty and bloodshed. And so, I understand it." He turned his attention back to the glass jar before he spoke again. Feeling the coolness of the glass as it encased the tragic Cora, he said, "But what shall we do with this poor little thing?"

"She can do no harm where she is. I'd like to leave her up here in this abode for now," Isra asserted. *A meaningless object to grace the kitchenette would be fitting for the time being,* she thought.

Astrid put a finger to his lips as he thought attentively about the commodity in front of him. "You know, it would be most unfortunate if something terrible should happen to that jar. One false motion and it would come crashing down, breaking into a million shattered pieces!" he jeered. A hideous look formed upon his face.

Isra found this oddly enchanting about him. They were both destructive in their own formidable way and yet she never felt threatened by him. They weren't competitive with each other. They were one of the same. She liked that. It gave the relationship she shared with him an edge, a quality that was supremely rare to find in any union between lovers.

Astrid seductively touched his lips with his tongue. A thought was brewing inside his head, that lovely, ornamental jar toppling beautifully from its pleasant place on the shelf, only to crash land onto the floor. A haphazard of its own, obliterated as it was reduced to crumbling fragments of nothing.

His thought flashed like an unrestrained fireball as a secretive smile resembled itself on his face like an apparition about to subside. *I know a witch who can do some terrible things,* he chuckled quietly to his ravenous mind. *I wonder if she will take the initiative. Hmm,* he chortled with a vile rapture.

Isra seemed to have picked on his sentimental mannerism as she allowed him to pull her closer as he leaned in for another cherished kiss reeking of ambrosia coated perfume.

"I am sure it would be most unfortunate if such violence was to commence!" Isra whispered, her eyes closed, in the middle of this succulent, savored kiss.

9

Ronald O'Kutte stood silently in the woods. His sword was positioned at his left side, glowing at him like a beacon in the fragrant morning sun. A faint whiff of cinnamon lingered on his breath. The spice still resided in his mouth from a very early morning breakfast.

He had been out in the clearing hiding under the sheltering trees. He focused on the glinting sharp point on his sword. He mused that it needed repair. He was a warrior at heart. It was in his birthright, but he had come to this part of the forest for a more delicate and yet personal reason.

Ronald was aiming for domination in his field of study. His goal in this instance was to be a warlock. He had been studying the magickal arts since the disappearance of his brother, Kane.

Legend said that the weak Kane had found himself entangled within the venomous claws of a witch. No tales could be told other than what the townspeople in Ronald's home village would say. The popular notion was that Kane had fallen prey to the dazzling witch's beauty and had either tragically died or escaped with his life, bringing great shame to his family name.

The consequence was nobody knew what happened to Kane

O'Kutte, but his brother Ronald had a pretty good inclination of where to start seeking an answer.

Ronald remembered the shouts and shrieks where the townspeople had often told tales of the unrighteous Lady Isra, a witch so unpleasant that her mere presence would send shivers down your spine. It was said she could make blood curdle and thicken in a foul-smelling conundrum! She had piercing green eyes that could detect any lie just by carefully examining her victim's body language. Those eyes could follow you everywhere! Villagers had the notoriety to stay away from Lady Isra, as would anyone who was considered even remotely sane.

Kane had heard the warnings about the fiery Lady Isra, but he had dreams of fortuitous greed and so those words given to him by his family and friends had fallen on deaf ears.

Ronald was much younger and yet so more managed in his sense of maturity. He was intelligent enough to know that such things known to be forbidden are those you should also give a wide berth. Ronald had only just turned sixteen when he had first heard those stories about the mighty witch, Lady Isra, but even then, he knew to steer clear!

Sadly, his brother Kane had not been as resourceful as Ronald. Kane had gone ahead and ignored all warnings, seeking out the witch for his own gains and nobody really knew what had happened to poor Kane O'Kutte.

Ronald was now nineteen years of age, a fine fellow with a vivid interest in the ways of magic and the occult. He knew exactly who Lady Isra was and had already made himself known to her. He would be doing more than that when the universe allowed.

He had great plans in store for the witch! However, for now, all he could do was admire the sun as it gently paraded its rays across the spaces between the trees, illuminating them through the cracks in which the light could sneak out and escape.

Ronald suddenly heard footsteps behind him. Perturbed by such an occurrence, he turned and spun around to face whoever it was that was soon to be in his presence. He was shocked as he found his eyes on a slender figure draped in blue velvet rich as midnight, the brightness of the material almost like a beacon in the dark, shadowy place.

The figure chuckled, clearly amused at Ronald's state of shock, and lifted her hood only to reveal gold glimmering hair in ringlets as eyes in bewitching, emerald green dominated her face.

"Sorry dear, I didn't mean to startle you!" Lady Isra chucked, clearly amused at Ronald's reaction to her entrance.

Ronald bowed his head respectively. "Please forgive me, my lady, for you did not startle me! I was simply not made aware that it was you." He wondered if she believed his unsavory performance. He thought it was too much, personally.

"I take very early morning walks," Isra explained cautiously as she carefully looked behind her then checked both sides of her direction before she proceeded to explain. "My lover isn't keen on me taking these early expeditions and adventures, so I have to check he's not following me as sometimes I just prefer my space despite the love that I share for my companion."

Ronald smiled. "I understand, my lady. I like my solitary time, too!" he expressed. "Say, how about we walk together? I'd like to ask you some questions if you feel able to answer them."

Isra looked at Ronald with much disdain wondering what such a mortal would want to know from her, but instead of allowing that venom to show up on their encounter, she simply smiled sweetly.

"Sure, why not? It would be nice to stroll with another!" the witch mused keenly.

Ronald walked slowly beside the witch. He didn't notice a raven lean in close as it rested itself upon a lingering tree branch. The raven watched closely as Isra and Ronald walked at a steady pace, talking in brief sentences. Its beady eyes were all over Isra as she exchanged amused glances with the mortal who, despite his rugged exterior, seemed to be able to rustle up an enchanting discussion with the witch who was clearly mesmerized by his young yet robust charms.

The raven examined the situation further as he flew along with these two as they walked some more. The raven raised his wings, exercising caution as he hovered just above Lady Isra's glowing white mass of hair. His eyes were effervescently unfaltering as they were transfixed on the witch, the beady yellow focusing on every inch of her!

Anyone would have thought this would have been Lady Isra's lover Astrid, but suddenly you could notice a small injury upon his left talon, a dense but yet closed cut that had long since healed. It didn't seem to bother him as he flew with ease, but now it was well known that this raven was not Astrid. It could have been no other than Astrid's brother, Silas.

Silas watched Isra carefully. His fierce, protective eye glided across the forest at Isra as she and Ronald found themselves entering a deserted clearing. No souls resided here as the ground was dry and forlorn. A dull brown color saturated it.

Isra was curious as she recognized the area but couldn't pinpoint from where she had seen it before. Her memory had carelessly run away with her! She ran her finger across the dusty ground and smirked. Nothing could grow here. Only desolate and deathly shadows lingered amongst the murky terrain.

Ronald didn't know how to react as he too felt a connection to this deserted place, but like the witch, he could not fathom how he was connected to it. It was peculiar and unnerving. He wasn't used to not being in control of the way he carried himself while he processed those thoughts.

He turned to the witch fearfully, a grim frown regaling across his face. "Please my lady, if we may, can we leave this place? It gives me an unsightly feeling that I am not comfortable with!"

Lady Isra smiled, noticing the wannabe warlock's insatiable fear. "Of course, you may leave!" she uttered. "I am going to stay for a while."

She mused him with a graceful stance as she felt a tree behind her, placing her hand on the trunk. The rough texture was tough on her delicate skin as the power of this unsightly place mesmerized the curious soul inside her. All Ronald could muster in return was a perplexed glance as Isra silently felt the waves of nature sinking into her auric body. Her eyes closed, her body dormant and silent as she sat wide awake under a transfixed way of being that only the universe could bestow!

He turned around before leaving to face the witch. His eyes were wide open, his brow relaxed, motioning a calm exterior as he departed. "I feel like I know you! I feel like you and I will get to be great friends." he said.

Lady Isra opened her left eye, not completely aware, but something inside of her was stirring. There was some familiarity in those words uttered by this majestic warrior, but even a formidable creature such as Isra could not attain directly what that familiar feeling would be.

Ronald swiftly bowed his head before he left the deserted clearing, leaving Isra in conversation with the tree.

IT WAS QUIET. The skies filled with black as a thousand stars twinkled at one another, wildly glinting up with possibility. The moon was almost full. Contessia could see it from the window frame as it shone from outside. The branches of the trees stood out with open arms, looking like silhouettes against the moon's glow.

Contessia was repeating words to herself as if in a rhyme or a passage. She didn't quite understand what she was doing. She felt in a delusional state most of the time, rambling to herself, not knowing if her words made sense.

"Soon, it will be time," she murmured to herself.

There was some significance in the word "soon," but Contessia was unable to figure out what that meant. Contessia had grown significantly since she had come to the tower. She didn't fully understand her situation of her having to be here until her very last day on earth and neither did she know the full story of how Lady Isra came to own her very soul, but she had accepted it. Contessia knew that Isra had gone to great lengths to protect her, but Isra hadn't let slip on how that had occurred and what she had done to ensure Contessia was protected.

Isra was very tight-lipped on everything, but Contessia knew Isra had claimed Contessia's soul in a bid to overcome her old foe Everilda, and as Contessia remembered Everilda, she knew she was a trickster. A bitter, old hag that couldn't live up to the power of Lady Isra and neither could she conquer her, that was Everilda. A failure in all things, as Isra put it. Contessia wasn't surprised when Lady Isra later told her the story of how she had finally defeated Everilda.

However, yet again this evening, Contessia was alone. It was a cool night. Summer was almost here. Spring had come in like a wave and it had felt like there had been little time for the flowers to bloom. She could barely make out their sweet fragrant scent when she went out into the tower grounds.

There will be a full moon in three days. Contessia could tell as the moon was almost filled up all the way. When the eve of the full moon dawned, that moon would be completely aglow in its opaque evanescence. She was staring at the moon when suddenly a sound from above started her.

"Contessa!" it called out! It was a female voice although Contessia was startled because she had expected to be alone.

Contessia looked around her. She couldn't see anyone else in the room so she found it odd because surely if a person was there calling her, she would at least notice them.

You've got my name wrong, she thought to herself, musing as she turned her head away. Bemused, she turned her attention back to the howling winds outside.

"Contessia, I mean, answer me! Look up!" the voice commanded, correcting herself since it knew they had gotten Contessia's name wrong at first.

Contessia stood surveying the area around her, wondering where this noise, this voice was coming from. Then she heard a tapping sound. It sounded like glass echoing from where she was standing.

A pounding sounded above Contessia's head, causing her to look up at the shelf positioned next to the window. All that Contessia could see was some glass bottles labeled with their contents, two glass jars as well as some ornate gold decorative statues. She couldn't see where the noise was coming from.

"Maybe I am crazy!" she voiced calmly. "Maybe I am imagining this!"

The pounding rang again, this time louder and with such violent force that it was surprising that whatever was making the bang didn't knock themselves onto the floor.

"You're not crazy! I know you can hear me!" the voice shrieked once more.

Contessia's eyes narrowed, focusing on the middle of the shelf. A turquoise jar glimmered at her. It appeared to have blue glitter inside but as Contessia looked closer, she could see a figure tapping furiously against the jar. Contessia didn't know who the occupant inside the jar was, but now she could clearly make out this tiny person banging against the glass walls of the jar, so desperate to make contact with her.

"Finally, you see me!" Cora shouted.

"Yes, I see you!" Contessia gasped, grabbing hold of the jar and examining it closely. "Although for a moment, I thought I was going insane."

Contessia peered inside, tempted to unscrew the lid. Her fingers were grasping it most forcefully. Cora saw this and looked cross as she shouted.

"No. Don't do that. Lady Isra enchanted it. If you unscrew it, I'll die," Cora begged.

Contessia could tell by the desperation in Cora's voice that she was being sincere.

"Why did Isra cast that spell upon you, placing you inside that thing?" Contessia asked.

"It's a long story. Lady Isra and I have known each other for a long time.," Cora began as she leaned closer to Contessia's face.

"Well, I have time. Do tell," Contessia muttered, sitting down on the cold stone floor and placing Cora's jar beside her so that both were at eye level.

"I first knew her when I was sixteen. She was younger then, but a man had just broken her heart and so she sought refuge to console herself by enlisting the dark ways! My father witnessed her as her heart blackened for the first time. He's seen darkness before, but nothing as dark as her!" Cora said.

She sat and folded her arms before continuing. "I wasn't allowed out after dark, but I had been careful to sneak away and I caught sight of her. I watched as black clouds dominated from above her. Lightning sparks lit up the night sky. Two huge dragons larger than anything I could imagine encircled both sides of her. Isra was positioned on a hilltop, not the one where her tower stands now, but another. I watched as her heart area inside her chest grew this blackened material over it. I can't even describe it, but it was so real. Like black mold clinging to her heart, surrounding the entrance to it. That was the night her soul became truly blackened."

Cora finished and stood once more, trying to gauge whether Contessia was on her side or Lady Isra's. The girl was forced by malevolent means to stay in Isra's tower so Cora knew it might be a challenge to get her onside, but getting Contessia to hear Cora's story was something Cora herself had not expected.

And Cora had so much more to tell, but where to begin? How would she tell this girl that she had Lady Isra hold claim to her soul by using magicks forbidden to her world in order to do that? How would Cora tell Contessia that she and Isra had poisoned Contessia's mind against the gnome she regarded as her friend?

Cora didn't know how to get into that subject and she felt tremendously guilty. Even while trapped in this jar for what she knew to be the remainder of her life, Cora had never wanted to summon those magicks. Cora had only done what Isra wanted because Isra had frightened Cora by threatening the life of Cora's father who was in exile. She would have been devastated if anything happened to her father, so she had shut her mouth and got on with the job at hand, pleasing Lady Isra. There was nothing else she could have done.

She stared at Contessia for what seemed like forever, noting this girl who had been dragged into something so deep didn't have an awareness of how badly stuck in it she truly was. Contessia was someone who was easily scared. You could barely startle Contessia and she'd shudder as if she was expecting some kind of lingering doom. Cora's shrieking had fired up Contessia's fear.

Could Cora rely on Contessia being calm if Cora had relayed the truth to her? That was a gamble Cora wasn't sure she could risk her life on. But Cora knew she was going to be trapped inside the jar unless Lady Isra undid the enchantment she had placed upon it or in the unlikely event that Isra died, as her magic would also die. The dying wasn't likely to commence, Cora had to be real with herself there. She'd have to settle for the truth and hope Contessia came around to her way of things.

Cora felt something inside her throat before opening her mouth. She felt incredibly nervous at having to tell Contessia what she knew but she also knew the only way in life to do any good was to tell the truth. "This isn't easy for me to say, girl, but I know the real circumstances of how Lady Isra came to own your soul!" she began.

Contessia's eyes narrowed; her brow raised as she tried to convince herself of such an idea. She knew Lady Isra would never manipulate her.

"What do you mean?" Contessia challenged, feeling extremely skeptical.

"Lady Isra asked me to help her. She came to my village asking for my assistance to claim a young girl's soul."

Contessia said nothing, just stared at Cora.

"She wouldn't say why or whose soul it was, telling me it wasn't my business to ask, but later during the trance, I saw everything. I saw you Contessia, and I so badly wanted to tell you, to break this hold she had on you, but by then it was too late." Cora re-imagined the color show of magic as she remembered her painful vision of Contessia.

"I'm not sure I believe you," Contessia replied. "Lady Isra has been good to me. Took me away from where I was and gave me a home."

Cora smirked in realization, almost laughing. "But Lady Isra didn't give you a home, dear. She took it. She saw you were young and weak and she yanked the floor from beneath your feet, placing you in this dire world where everything is her own. That's what she does."

"I was placed in some garish things, but that was her lover Astrid," Contessia said in defense.

"Astrid did those things to you, yes. But I can guarantee you Lady Isra knew what he was doing. Then there's the matter of your friend, the gnome?" Cora asked as she felt brave to broach the subject.

"Oh, Klinq? He's not my friend," Contessia snorted coolly.

"That right there is my point!" Cora said, almost snapping. She felt frustrated, slowly losing her patience, fearing that Contessia wasn't going to believe a single syllable that came from her mouth. "He was your friend. He tried to do all he could to protect you despite his own fears overwhelming him. Lady Isra saw that, and she used it. She had me cast a spell in which you forgot he was your friend!"

This truly was the clincher. The golden eagle was about to land on a field, triumphantly having succeeded, or in the alternative that Contessia didn't believe, it was about to fall down, having lost its ability to fly.

"Hmmm," Contessia replied before sitting up straight. Her eyes closed as if she was in a meditative state, calm and focused.

All Cora could do was look on and wonder. After a few minutes, Contessia stood up, almost on a whim, but in a moment's pause she returned her attention to the window, grabbing Cora's jar along with her as she proceeded to stand beside it. Admiring the night sky and the brilliant stars shining back in amongst the darkness, they seemed to calm her, give her inspiration, some kind of courage as if she had been able to process the information given to her and now seeming a lot calmer.

"I'm not saying I believe you, but there is a lot of amiss here. I'd like to talk to my sister first before we enter into anything."

"Okay," Cora swallowed. "In order for me to be set free, Lady Isra has to be the one who reverses the spell and as you can see, I'm in here until she decides to do that. I have nothing to lose by saying this to you. I'm risking a lot by even mentioning it."

"I understand," Contessia mouthed, "but my sister Isra has been through a change since her death and if I can find her reasoning, perhaps I can get her to set you free." She felt confident that she could get Isra to change her mind.

Cora was hesitant. "Okay, but I could never believe Lady Isra could ever be anything but evil! It's all she knows."

"When she came back from her perishment, something in her changed. I know it's hard for you to believe but I know what I see in her eyes. It's not hate or malice anymore. There is good in there," Contessia finished as she turned once more to the window.

10

Astrid paced frantically. The raven-man was filled with anxiety as his feet hit the floor continuously with a solid thud. Silas had not long got back from his expedition in the forest where he had been witness to Lady Isra conversing with a man. Astrid was a little annoyed as Silas had lost sight of Isra because she had gone too far down in the undergrowth of the forest terrain for him to keep track of her.

Silas had reported back to Astrid with what he had observed, flying into the tower, telling his brother exactly what he had seen! Despite Silas's efforts to reassure Astrid, they fell deathly silent to the raven-man's hearing. He was worried for Isra and he was more worried that Silas had not been able to keep up with her. Of course, he knew Isra was well versed with the forest terrain and she knew it memorably, having spent many years in the green felled woods. She had a deep knowledge of every creature and being that dwelled there.

Astrid didn't know what he was more upset about, that Silas had managed to lose Isra or that she had not yet arrived back at the tower as it was now several hours later. The night was making its way in as grey clouds dominated the weary skies.

Surely, she should have been back home by now, he thought pensively.

His feet still paced across the stone floor as his mind wandered as to exactly where his love could be. He presumed she would be arriving home at any moment, but his mind was overtaking him, thinking of every dire possibility it could manifest!

Astrid was not concerned over Isra's actuality of conversing with another male, but he was bothered about the identity of this strange male figure that had suddenly been prominent in introducing himself to the witch in such a short period. It was bemusing to Astrid as to why a human, a human interested in magic no less, would want to have business with Isra! Naturally he was predicting the worst.

Astrid's thoughts were interrupted when a slam of a door brought his pacing to a grand halt. Footsteps eagerly approached as the sound grew closer. The steps grew louder as the precedent made its way upward. Feet hammered across the floor as they maintained a steady pace climbing up the twisted staircase.

Astrid held a small pause as the steps grew closer. Clicking his fingers, he looked confidently at the door as it opened. A vision in midnight blue stepped through it, pushing the hood of her majestic cloak down as she giggled at Astrid's confused look.

Astrid looked at Isra, mystified that he had been able to note that she would be home at any moment and sure enough, she had arrived moments after! Had he manifested this? He had become very adept at the magickal arts, but it wasn't his intention to bring her to him in such an unorthodox manner! Just thinking of the idea sent swirls of rapid energy, shooting up and all around him as he did his best to digest and take in the shock of what he had done.

Isra reached out to hug her beloved companion and upon seeing he was still confused having a bemused look splashed across his face, she giggled again.

"Oh my, dear Astrid, why do you look so solemn, love?" Isra cackled, amusement resounding all over her cheeks.

He sighed, shrugging his shoulders as he looked at her longingly. "It's nothing, really."

Isra's retaliating glance was one of perplexity and intrigue. She knew he was lying, but she wasn't going to brace the subject any further. He was anxious about her being gone but he didn't have the spawn to confront her about it. She ventured to open her mouth to speak but she was stopped as a finger firmly pressed against her lips, gently silencing her.

Astrid worked his way down her body, lifting that brilliant blue velvet cloak away from her as he rubbed her thighs tenderly, anticipating the arousal as he softly made his way down, stopping a little as his tender kisses planted themselves just before her legs. He looked at her in eager desire as he spread her legs, looking up at her, a smile on his face emerging as he gazed at her with such devotion.

With just his hands, he maneuvered himself up to her lips, pressing his chest into hers. The blue cloak crashed to the floor in a heap as it peeled off her body, revealing a lace bodice in white hugging her body as Astrid drank Isra in, taking in every facet of her. His tongue spontaneously massaged hers with a circular motion, tasting her, filling him up with her.

He wasn't allowing himself the freedom to breathe. He just kept going. He found himself drenched in his vibrant desire for her, to be close to her. Just the feeling of his skin touching hers was sending vibrational shivers down his back, running rampant as they cascaded down to his lower regions, filling his manly parts with gratified pleasure.

Softly she moaned while he distractingly undid the buttons of her lace bodice, discarding the unwanted garment to the floor as he resumed his passion for her. His lips touched hers as he could taste fragrant strawberries on them, reminding him of summer. Her lips clasped onto his as he forced her up against the ornate door, holding her in place as he mounted her. Stifled moans could be heard as he lunged inside her, pushing into her core as he caressed her chest. His eyes closed so he was fully in the moment.

Silas looked upon them in a passionate embrace, smirking. "It looks like you are busy, dear brother. I will be back soon." And with that he flew out of the open window, disappearing into the night.

~

SILAS SCANNED the ground from above. He was in flight, having only left the tower of Astrid and Isra not that long ago. Lady Isra and Astrid were getting down to romantic business, so he had swiftly exited the scene.

The cover of night prevented him from seeing properly as it did during the day. The raven wasn't as young and sprightly as he used to be and his eyesight often failed him. He had to examine a subject at close range to know precisely what it was.

The raven's eyes were fixated on the grass, checking for any sudden movement on the terrain below. His mind was focused on food gathering as it was the late hours, and he hadn't had a decent worm in a good few hours. His stomach rumbled, indicating his need to feed. He laughed in response as food was exactly what he had on the agenda. He just had to lunge upon his prey before he would get to tuck in. His stomach was impatient, having waited all night for Silas to feed his hunger.

Silas continued scanning the grass looking for any desirable food source. He caught sight of a black blob moving slowly. Its back was arched as in a defense position. A black cylinder weaved out of the grass like a snake in the wind. Silas couldn't determine what it was, so he swooped down to get a closer look. Silas launched himself downwards to land beside the mysterious black figure that he hoped would fulfill his nutritional need. He was ever so hungry.

He landed upon the soft, damp grass to be greeted by a black cat. The cat was staring at him with wild anticipation, giving Silas the once over. Silas paused. This cat was Onyx, the pet that belonged to Isra and Astrid, although he had suspected it was more Isra's familiar than Astrid's.

Well, that's my dinner gone, Silas chuckled to himself.

He would not be snacking upon the cat now that he knew whom it was. He didn't know Onyx very well, but he simply could not consume a family member, no matter how hungry he was. He was also sure he had seen that cat only a few minutes ago before he had left the tower.

That's odd, he paused to himself. He figured that the cat would ignore him and run off but instead Onyx sniffed Silas carefully.

"Hisssssssss," Onyx shrieked.

"Oh, come now," Silas said. "I'm not going to eat you. I might be a hunter by nature but I simply cannot consume one that I know to be family. We ravens do have some honor, you know," he said as he stood over Onyx, getting a good look at the cat.

"Oh, honor?" Onyx squeaked. "That's a fine thing if you happen to know what it is."

"Now, young man. Why would you come out with something like that? You're simply a little cat, or have I missed something?" Silas quizzed.

"I'm sorry, but I didn't ask for this life. Lady Isra is good to me. She feeds me and looks after me like I am her own child, but that Astrid ... well, he's ghastly. He's sometimes nice, feeding me scraps but Isra is the one I care about."

Silas was very bemused. This was a bizarre notion coming from a cat of all creatures. He pictured them to be very domestic animals but clearly with young Onyx, there was more to him than what was seen at first glance.

"In my day, cats would just be cats. They'd sit around the fire having themselves a tasty mouse in the quiet away from the humans, but maybe times have changed since I've been around. I am an old raven in these ages," Silas retorted.

He found it odd that Onyx was not only speaking to him but talking to him about honor, something a cat wouldn't have any knowledge of.

"I used to have honor," the cat replied, licking his lips at Silas as if he was viewing the old bird as a morsel he was about to pounce on any second from now.

"I'm sure you did," Silas responded, using his right wing to scratch his head, baffled at this conversation he was having with another animal. He knew that only humans spoke about such important matters so he really was questioning all he could right now.

He didn't know what to say to Onyx. This cat was perturbed and confused about its existence. Silas observed that Onyx didn't understand the way of things. Cats were supposed to laze around, eating plentiful helpings of scraps. Silas felt quite peculiar at having a conversation with a cat that didn't behave like a cat. Neither did he sound like one.

"But then I was brought to this life and all honor I had was gone. Well admittedly, it was gone before then, but this life vanquished all hope of claiming it back," Onyx said.

Silas watched Onyx closely. He seemed to be staring at something in the grass. The cat had its paws positioned together, eyes glowing like that of a hawk waiting for the right moment when it would dive at its prey. In this instance, whatever Onyx was focused on had run away. The cat's focus came right back to Silas.

"I am out here to try to eat, but with you here, I have no chance of doing that. You're scaring all my food away!" he moaned, annoyed at the bird's presence distracting him from his hunt.

"I am sorry," Silas mouthed. "Say, wouldn't you be more comfortable at home tucked up upon a warm blanket, digging into a nice scrap of meat?" he questioned Onyx.

"I would, only my mistress is getting very personal attention from the man of the house. And therefore, she is too busy to fetch me meat," Onyx responded.

This brought a smile to Silas's face. He too had left the tower on this night because of Astrid and Isra getting intimate with each other. Silas was going to speak to Astrid before going out on his hunt but since his brother was getting sweaty with Isra, Silas had decided to leave that discussion for another time.

"Ah, yes. My brother. He's a funny old soul. I don't know how he happened to end up with a witch of all beings, although he seems happy with her," Silas jokes.

"Happy is one way of saying it," Onyx countered.

Silas chuckled. "You know, for a cat, you seem very unhappy.

Please do tell me what is troubling you. Maybe I can help," Silas suggested.

"I don't think you can help me," came Onyx's reply.

He sounded angry and frustrated. His back arched once more as if he had enough questioning and helpful suggestions from the charismatic raven.

"I really do not know, young man, but honestly, for a little furry thing placed in a privileged way of life, you sound so dire. It makes one wonder what became of such a happy creature."

"I was happy once, but then I messed it up."

And with that Onyx skulked off, disappearing back into the dark cover of night. Silas was dumbfounded. He had no clue over what to say to make this situation better. Onyx was indeed puzzling to the old raven. Silas was starting to suspect that something wasn't quite right with this fur-brained animal.

He decided not to probe the subject any further but what he had observed was spine-tingling to say the least. Silas could feel it in his bones. Something was not as it seemed to be.

11

A gnome shuffled around in the undergrowth as the moon shone down. He raised a furrowed brow as the light came into his line of vision, causing him to place a hand on his head, feeling self-conscious. An owl hooted in the tree next to him.

"Be quiet!" he chortled, fearing he would be discovered.

Klinq wasn't supposed to return to Shambre Fell. He shouldn't be hiding in the grass in the midnight winds. He knew that. That raven-man Astrid had banished him under the witch Lady Isra's name. Klinq thought that was odd, but still he was so terrified, he'd fled without looking back.

Klinq had left behind his dear friend Contessia but felt so guilty that he could not back her up and defend her honor although Klinq couldn't understand her reasoning of why she had allowed that to happen. He presumed it was a spell when he witnessed her turn away from him in disgust.

He knew things had been really rough between him and Contessia. He hadn't been able to stand up for her after all that had happened to her when she first came to the tower of Isra and Astrid, and then when she became Isra's protégé, Klinq fled from the tower, crawling to Isra's nemesis Everilda in the dark of night.

73

Klinq was in a ghastly plight, caught in the battle of two witches: Everilda wanting to conquer Isra and Isra determined to see Everilda fail, rubbing Everilda's nose in it as much as she could. Enter Contessia into the fold, dragged into things by Everilda who saw her as a pawn, and he was really in quite the hot mess.

In the midnight glow of the moon, Klinq had pleaded with Everilda to set Contessia free, begging her to be left out of her horrid plan only to have his words fall on deaf ears as Everilda knew an asset where she saw one. She wasn't going to let Contessia off while Contessia was at the center of Isra's world. There was no chance of that.

So Klinq walked away feeling defeated, having not only lost Contessia, but he had also failed in his attempt to save her from being dragged into this dark, bitter battle. Now he was a lone man, well not a man, but he was alone in the wilderness, banished and exiled by the fiery raven-man Astrid, Lady Isra's counterpart in the witch's absence.

Klinq didn't take anything, holding his head down as he fled, running as far as his tiny gnome legs would carry him. And here he was in the forest at night, preparing to return.

Some would have questioned his sanity, wanting to come back to a place he had been strictly forbidden never to come back to, however Klinq saw the obstacles and some part of him hoped that Isra could be forgiving to his plight, but he knew Astrid wasn't. The raven-man was bold and courageous, always standing up for what he believed to be right even when he was found to be in the wrong. But still, Klinq yearned for acceptance.

It was getting closer to dawn. The moon shimmered aglow, ready to greet the wholesome sun. Klinq sighed, exhaling his fear as he stood up, reaching for his shoulder bag. It was time for him to make his move, bravely entering that ghastly tower to face his fate.

How bad could it really be? he pondered.

He had nothing to lose. Everything he wanted he had already lost, so really when it came down to it, Klinq had nothing.

~

THE SUN glimmered in Klinq's eyes. The light blinded him as the orange entity glowed ferociously in the morning light.

He had left the protection of the wild undergrowth, taking this journey before dawn to get back to the place that stood before him, on the hilltop looking abundant in its many hues of rich green. Beyond that just surrounding the area was a delicate stream. He hadn't noticed it before, but it went around Shambre Fell, running down around the tower and then continuing to flow past inviting trees before dipping down into the forest.

Then he saw the tower, normally a black silhouette as it beckoned among the vastest areas of the land, but today it was covered in light. The black was not so present anymore as he looked up to find himself staring into the tallest part of the tower, a gold gilded window frame in his view.

"Perhaps it's just my vision. It is early!" he said to himself, dismissing the lightness of the tower as an illusion as he plundered on ahead, inching steadily through the green grass blades.

Pink roses decorated the grounds, presumably planted after winter had ended. Klinq didn't recall seeing them before. He hadn't been able to remember seeing much of the way of flora around Shambre Fell during his short stay there.

Klinq found himself possessed with ideals of what good and evil should be, although he knew what good was as he had once been it, kind, giving and caring. But then he had aligned himself with dark witches, tainting his once good name. But wicked was truly wicked. Once you go bad, you cannot go back.

The perplexity of the thing was Klinq was not able to accept what he saw, that the tower was shrouded in light. He had expected it to be in its former inky black, but now it seemed to show shades of gray with beige and white in between. It was rather profound, but he could only put it down to the witch emerging in the witch, but then how can such a thing be? He pondered mindlessly as he raced to the tower door.

He felt startled as he pushed the ornate oak door open, trembling as his feet were unsteady behind him. He heard voices coming from the floor above, shrieks of laughter from a female and then a mocking voice that Klinq assumed was the male counterpart of Isra's, Astrid.

He started to climb that complicated staircase, twisting and unwinding in its soft silvery gray where fate would lead him to his doom. Klinq had almost reached the top, just about to place his foot onto the last step, when a black mass appeared beside him. The black entity unfolded its wings as Klinq shuddered, realizing it was a raven.

"Do not be afraid, small man. I have no desire to nourish myself with a gnome," he called out hastily.

Klinq went back two steps, inching himself as if he was preparing for an escape. Then he realized it wasn't the voice of Astrid. It was different, less harsh. Softer in tone with that of a kind and endearing heart, a trait that wasn't known for the raven turned man, Astrid.

"Wait, you're not him!" Klinq stuttered in amazement. "But if you're not him and I know that is true, then who are you?!"

The raven bowed his head. "Oh, I am sorry! I thought you knew. My name is Silas. I am Astrid's brother."

Klinq took another step back, fearing that something unspeakable was going to happen. Silas understood why the gnome was in such a great panic and he knew better than anyone that nothing could be accomplished with sheer panic and violence. He looked at Klinq with disdain and frowned at the gnome.

"Do not fear me. I am not here to make your life a more miserable existence than it already is. I cannot speak for Astrid and his counterpart, but I will not harm you in any way," Silas explained.

Klinq was considering what Silas had said. His head turned to the right side as he pondered the raven's words carefully, although he found he had difficulty in distinguishing why someone related to that dreadful man Astrid would be kind and good. That was a disturbing realization for Klinq!

"You've risked great peril to come here again!" Silas uttered.

Klinq said nothing. He kept his head down, ashamed of himself and the way things had played out for him here.

"It's not up to me to judge you, but I've heard their conversations regarding your name. They think I don't hear, but I do," Silas muttered. He changed his tone as he turned to Klinq. "Do tell me, are there any juicy worms in the earth today? I fancy myself a snack! It's not that I hate the food here, but I do like a good, tasty worm. The way they slither in your throat as you gobble them whole as they slide down is a wonderful feeling. My goodness, my friend, you just can't beat it!" Silas carried on.

Klinq didn't really know what to say. He hadn't expected a friendly chat with a raven. A conversation regarding tasty, succulent worms had not been on the forefront of his mind either.

"I am not too sure," Klinq answered. "I've not seen any."

Silas smiled, realizing Klinq didn't have an answer for him. He stretched his wings, standing on his claws, ready to take flight.

"I'd be best checking out the earth's larder for myself then. I'm bound to find one if I look in the right places," he commented.

Before Klinq could respond, Silas swiftly maneuvered upwards, placing his attention toward a wide open window before he landed on the ledge, venturing into the warm, sunny skies. Klinq mumbled something to himself as he climbed that final step, preparing to meet his fate. The large door swung open and as Klinq expected himself to be the dim room with just a couch and a delicate window frame, surrounded with a small kitchenette, but he found himself in an elegant throne room.

Klinq's eyes darted to the back of the room where he glanced toward Lady Isra on a chair gilded in solid gold. Her shimmery white hair shone down before her, her arms rested on the support of the chair as the rest of her was delicately fashioned in purple silk.

Isra's eyes met Klinq's with a harsh frown. "It seems that the words 'banished' and 'forbidden' are lost beyond your comprehension, Sir Klinq," she emitted the tiniest hint of humor.

Klinq bowed his head toward the witch, bending himself down to greet her presence. "Yes, your regalness, I am so very sorry for that."

The witch waved a firm hand in his direction as a very familiar face appeared beside her, watching Klinq with his attentive vision. "Silence! I have no time for your pleasant duplicity," she barked.

"You were banished in my name so one must wonder why you'd have the idea to return?" she questioned, although by the way she glanced at Astrid and in turn he smiled at her then wickedly toward Klinq, he guessed it wasn't really a question.

"I came to earn my reprieve, and one hopes your forgiveness," Klinq said carefully, noting his use of words and the tone in which he spoke them. Just one mistake could be the end for him if he wasn't cautious.

Isra seemed to consider his request She turned her head to the side before turning to Astrid who had his hands rubbed together as if awaiting a great morsel of delicious food. The food in Astrid's ideal vision would be the notion of having his way with the terrified gnome. She then turned her attention to Astrid who had yet another wicked grin plastered across his face.

Oh, what he would do to that short gnome if he'd had his chance. The terrible acts he'd be serving would be that of pure malice and nothing else. How she'd relish watching that. Her eyes found themselves staring into Astrid's bold eye sockets before she turned away again as if in some sort of thought.

Astrid saw this vivid fascination but still he wasn't moving away from this most scrumptious idea of his. He felt the wickedness of it pulsing through his veins. He had banished this vile creature of course and with great pleasure, so to do what he pleased with Klinq would be right on top of a list of things that would make Astrid enormously happy.

Astrid looked at Klinq with a wicked smile, quickly turning to Isra. "Let me have this vile creature. Let me destroy every feeble inch of him," he barked, almost spitting with excitement as he watched Klinq closely.

"Calm yourself, Astrid," Isra commanded, noting her lover's enthusiasm. "It is no consequence that our dear Klinq is in a lot of trouble, but I will spare him." She glanced at the gnome's face as he awaited her judgment.

"Oh, thank you, Lady Isra," Klinq responded, his hands pressed together and held close to his face. He looked up from his position on the floor and stared at her, and then his relieved smile disappeared, only to be replaced with putrid fear.

Isra put her finger to her lips before she spoke. Her eyes narrowed with the gnome's, inciting fear into his soul. "Not so fast, you coward! Where shall we begin with the injustices you have committed? Oh. Let's start with coming into my tower under false pretenses to gain knowledge. Of course, we must not forget the matter of conspiring against me with Everilda. Last of all, you were banished from the lands. You come back, knowing disastrous consequences would follow if you ever returned! I believe Sir Klinq is in a lot of hot water," she joked thoughtfully.

She turned to Astrid. "He has paid enough for his crimes, and I don't think Contessia would benefit from his presence, don't you agree?"

Astrid looked down at the gnome, nodding but saying anything.

"Very well," Isra replied. "I don't want you here, Klinq. You can go freely but this time, do not come back! For I warn you, next time I won't be so lenient."

Klinq looked ashamed, his mouth moving to voice inaudible words but before he could speak, Isra started again, looking down on him from where she beckoned. "If I catch you in an eye's distance from Contessia, I will allow Astrid to tear you to shreds." She laughed. "You'll have to excuse my dear Astrid's excitement. You see, he's not had a decent brawl in a while and he's hungry for the game. I know he is just anticipating the opportunity. If you disobey me, I will let him do as he wishes."

Astrid rubbed his hands together with a sly smile, grinning so widely Isra found he often reminded her of a young puppy, disobedient but still keen to earn rewards for good behavior although there was very little of that to be seen. Isra surveyed Astrid's yearning to rip Klinq apart. She found it quite passionate. Such violence in a man. It was thrilling to her.

She turned to Klinq, laughing again. "And that is the exact reason why I will let him. I could enact wondrous feats of cruelty upon you, but seeing Astrid have his way with you would give me so much pleasure."

"I see," Klinq started, rubbing a cloth-covered finger down his chin in a thoughtful pause. "But why may I not see Contessia?"

Lady Isra laughed once more, shooting a finger toward Klinq, reminding him that he was in her realm now. Anyone who could see with their eyes open could see Isra had grown attached to Contessia and as far as she saw it Klinq was scum, whether romantic feelings had grown between Contessia and the gnome was of no interest to Isra. He'd stay away and he'd better, or she'd take care of him.

Isra supposed she was softening in her old age, although the tender age of thirty-two was far from old, but she felt old in her soul. In some way, she felt like Contessia had known each other for hundreds of years, but how could that be when Contessia was barely twenty-two and Isra almost approaching her thirty-third year?

"Contessia is a dear, vulnerable soul and I will not allow you to confuse her in her weakened state." Isra stated sharply. "That is all. Astrid, escort our unwelcome guest out!"

Astrid was about to carry out his task when something came crashing up the staircase, startling everyone at once.

12

A black cat hissed and growled as it made its entrance into the grand throne room. Isra smiled as she noticed Onyx come in although she was feeling an inclination to ask why he was in such a tantrum.

Onyx was not a happy cat. His fur stood up on end as if he had been electrocuted, his tail wagging in the air with anger as he strode over to his mistress, Isra. She tenderly stroked the animal, whispering sweet things inside his ear in an attempt to calm him down. She had no idea why he was so worked up. He had a happy home, a warm loving mistress and master who fed him regularly and tended to his every need, and here he was making a scene over and his owners had no knowledge why.

Astrid hastily retreated in the direction of Klinq, forcing the gnome from his position and dragging him toward the door before Isra noticed something in the raven-man that she hadn't seen before. He was sweating. His forehead was covered in it. It wasn't normal for Astrid to exhibit signs of anxiety, so she found this rather perplexing but nevertheless, she allowed Astrid to take Klinq out of her abode.

She would raise the matter of what she saw with him later.

~

ISRA WALKED TOWARD THE WINDOW. It seemed she was in a trance as she was drawn to the land before her. The lush green that surrounded Shambre Fell in its entire majestic furor glimmered at her as she found herself staring down at the flowing stream. As she looked further, she saw the plantation of trees that led deep into the forest but as she looked closer, she found herself staring at an open space, all dormant and alone.

A door slammed shut, startling the witch and at once her trance was broken. Isra looked over to see who had shut the door and her eyes met Contessia's in a striking glance. Contessia had her head bent, ashamed and remorseful. Her eyes were narrowed and not really wanting to greet Isra's piercing green ones, but then Isra saw Contessia look at the shelf toward the back of the room.

Contessia pointed at it wildly as she watched with vivid curiosity. "That jar, it keeps talking to me. It keeps saying all kinds of horrid things about you!" she began.

Isra smiled at Contessia, almost smirking. "Jars tend to do that, dear. Worry not, for I know this particular jar won't be around for much longer!"

Contessia watched as Isra strode over to the wooden shelf that hung above the pantry where all the kitchenware could be found. Isra picked up the sparkling blue jar, tapping her fingers at its sides as a tiny girl inside, banged at it, kicking the glass walls as the glitter specks tumbled down in a desperate attempt to break free.

"You see," Isra continued as she held the jar, "this is a very precious little thing, and we all know glass especially breaks ever so easily. All you need is one vital swoop. Just one knock and our little friend here and her glass home could shatter to a million pieces."

Contessia looked down at the jar, staring at Cora who stood helplessly inside it. "Yes, dear sister. I see what you mean, but why would she tell me you trapped her in there?"

"Perhaps she is just desperate for attention. I did trap her in there, but it was her own reward for mocking me," Isra remarked as she placed the girl and the jar upon the shelf. "Anyhow, I would not worry yourself. She won't be a decorative house ornament for long," Isra whispered with a smile.

Contessia looked taken aback. She was trying to understand why a girl was trapped inside this jar in the first place; surely there were more humane acts of punishment, but Contessia didn't always understand why Isra did the things she did.

"She says you trapped her inside because you didn't want her telling anyone about the bargain you two made!" Contessia remarked, feeling out of place in this wilderness. Despite Isra's transformation from dark to light, she still felt her sister's heart very much resided within the dark realms.

"I did," Isra replied.

"But why?" Contessia asked, feeling sympathetic towards the trapped girl.

Isra looked over toward Contessia, noting the sadness in her eyes. *Aha,* she thought! *I see what's going on here! Cora has attempted to manipulate my dear, sweet Contessia with a delicate sob story. Of course, she is the victim in every scenario she presents herself in.* Isra chuckled malevolently to herself.

"The girl was a menace, dear. She bargained with me before and has always been known for her trickery. I simply enacted what many have been too scared to do! No longer is this sweet looking child with bulging blue eyes tormenting innocents, fooling them into debauchery with her wicked ways! Now she's nicely tucked away, no longer able to deceive or create pretty lies!" Isra replied.

Contessia looked away, almost lingering away from Isra's sight as she found herself wondering just what torrid things Isra and Cora delved in back in the time when they knew each other. Understanding that both Isra and Cora's stories were similar in nature, she knew both were likely to be telling their own kind of truths, but perhaps also masking some aspects of that truth.

Contessia really didn't want to raise the matter, but this was why she had come here to ask her dear sister for Cora's release, so she whispered, "And you wouldn't consider setting her free?"

"That depends," Isra remarked. "Has our Cora learnt her life-long lesson, or is there more for her to learn? Maybe she should consider whether her life is better encased in glass."

"I see," Contessia decided, realizing that Isra was adamant regarding her choice ... for now, at least. "But would you consider it?" Contessia asked once more.

Isra took a moment, eying Contessia carefully, wondering what had caused the girl to be so darn curious, always asking this and wanting to know that. She was a wide-open book full of knowledge, yearning to know the possibilities of life. Contessia would always try to see both sides before making a judgment and despite her somewhat deluded personality, Isra liked that about Contessia. It gave her some diplomacy which Isra rarely saw in those beings that considered themselves lightworkers.

"If I deemed it to be right, then yes. I would consider it. Whatever gave you the notion to ask, child?"

"Just something I've seen in you lately. You're different than when we first met and in my short but detailed conversation with Cora, I believe she deserves a chance. Not much of a chance, but a chance still."

Isra straightened, lowering her glance. "You're a kind and giving soul, Contessia. I hope for your sake you never let someone use that against you, for it could be your undoing. I will most undoubtedly consider your request, but for now I must retire. I seem to slumber more since I almost left this reality."

Isra held her dress close to her as she turned to the stairs, looking behind her as she saw a small smile appear on Contessia's face. And for some unknown reason, Isra smiled back.

ASTRID TURNED to Klinq as he shut the oak ornate door behind him. He had escorted the gnome down the stone staircase and now was about to give him a stern warning to never come back. He had banished Klinq before and thought it was quite brave and also stupid for the gnome to come back after all he had said to him before. As far as Astrid was concerned, Klinq was in for a severe reprimand.

However, Astrid wasn't his usual self. The raven-man was acting rather off-color. He was acting very anxious as his and Isra's cat Onyx stormed into the throne room, and although Isra noticed his behavior, she had no clue what was going on in that head of his.

Klinq wasn't as stupid as he looked which might have come as a shock to some, as many thought him to be as dumb as a post. Klinq looked at Astrid as they stood facing one another. He noticed Astrid's face as well as the beads of sweat dripped down past his forehead and onto his nose. Astrid tried to straighten himself out and maintain his firm, booming attitude but he wasn't fooling Klinq.

"You're sweating a lot, Astrid. The way I come to see it, that's one of the symptoms of your lies coming to get you!" Klinq observed.

"I didn't ask for advice from a cowardly gnome who can't stay away from the place he was banished from!" Astrid snapped, wiping away more sweat from his brow.

Klinq lowered his stance, feeling sympathetic to the raven-man for the very first time. "No, you didn't ask, but I'm going to give it to you anyway. As a gnome who has gotten the bad end of many witches, all I can say is whatever you are keeping from her, don't do it for too long because the longer you keep this from her, the worse it will get when she discovers the truth," Klinq warned.

"Thanks, but I'm not about to join the ranks of the lonely gnome parade," Astrid countered sarcastically. Astrid got close to Klinq's face, folding his arms up at Klinq, feeling both anxious and intimidated by this gnome who seemed to know it all and suddenly wasn't afraid of Astrid anymore.

He thought, *How dare you psychoanalyze me when we both know you are a coward who can't stand up for his so-called friend. Yes, I know what you are. Foolish little man! You have no comprehension of why I do the things I do, so do us both a favor and mind your own business,* Astrid thought with a loud grunt.

Klinq heard the grunt but didn't realize what the raven-man was thinking. If Klinq had a spine, he'd have challenged it, but Klinq didn't possess the guts needed to pursue a confrontation. Klinq didn't know Astrid too well.

He thought of Astrid as an awful being that made him tremble if he was within an inch of him, but in that throne room, just seeing the raven-man's behavior after Astrid had witnessed the way that dreadful cat was behaving, Klinq had noticed weakness in Astrid. How he managed to uncover it, he wasn't sure but just watching Astrid when that cat came in all puffed up and angry spoke volumes to Klinq. You'd think a man with Astrid's strength and masculine presence would have been able to keep it hidden. But sadly, no. It had emerged right in front of Klinq's eyes much to Astrid's revulsion.

"You don't know why I'm doing this," Astrid said, feeling defensive. "She is not to know! Not in this universe. Never." Astrid waved a finger in Klinq's direction, harshly commanding him to keep his gob shut.

Nobody knew the things Astrid did, the lengths he had to go to just to keep things quiet. He was very cloak-and-dagger about it. He'd do anything to just keep it low key and out of view from prying eyes. You see, Astrid had been keeping things a secret from Isra almost since the beginning, and now that someone knew Astrid was keeping something from her, he was beginning to sweat over it.

If she ever found out... he thought. *She'd leave me or worse, hate me and throw it in my face how I lost her for all eternity. That would be a fate worse than death.* He'd sooner be tortured for all time. He could take the torture from her, but he'd never want to be on the receiving end of her hatred. That would be far too much for him to bear.

Klinq relented, dropping his shoulders as he turned away from Astrid. "I guess I'll be on my way but I have to say, if this is your way of protecting her, the truth is a more likely friend than an enemy."

And with that, Klinq walked off feeling both relieved and troubled. But he knew he could never set foot in Shambre Fell again. It would simply be too dangerous to do so.

13

Astrid quietly opened the door to his and Isra's bedroom. He stood quiet as a mouse as he watched her. She was sitting at her dresser combing her long fair hair. She meticulously focused on each golden curl as it fell loosely against her back. Isra donned a white lace nightgown, open at the back revealing a partial layer of skin. That soft peach tempted him from afar, glaring at him.

Astrid tried to maintain his silent stance as his hunger for her grew. Just seeing the image of her so undressed was enough to topple him. He couldn't control himself around her. She had a magnetizing energy that sent sparks down his spine. The electricity surged through his brain as he tried to contain his irrational thoughts.

Isra placed the comb down on the dresser and spun around, facing her counterpart. One would be inclined to say that Isra knew Astrid had been there. She was quite perceptive when you observed she had her back turned to him, tempting him from afar with her glorious beauty.

It was peculiar she hadn't said something sooner. Isra was the quiet type. She'd lay back and await you to come in, tired and forlorn then when you could no longer stand it. She'd go in, catching you while you stumbled on your lies and deceitful behaviors.

Astrid's eyes met hers, those green spectating eyes of hers glowering at him with sheer delight. She said nothing. Astrid didn't know what to say. He looked like he was about to crack under the pressure. Her sinister silence deafened him, forcing him to admit that which he knew he had been hiding from his love.

He thought she might question him as to how long he had been there. She gazed at him thoughtfully as if she was examining every part of him. He felt exposed under her glare. Astrid's cheeks turned the color of cherries. His face dropped. He felt like she was reading him. How could a person so close to him be able to uncover every last ghastly secret locked inside his soul? He felt panicked, considering the idea that she had rumbled him. Oh gosh, if she had, he'd be in for a scolding!

"Why so solemn, dear?" she remarked. She was sweet and sincere. Nothing evil laid in her demeanor. She smiled and draped her hand across her thigh, beckoning him to come over to her. She was subtle, luring him over.

Astrid was anxious. *Okay, so she hasn't caught me. She doesn't know. Goodness knows what I'd do if she did, but she hasn't.*

He relaxed a little and came close to her, dropping his arms at his sides. He had to stop this. What was he so afraid of? She didn't suspect a thing. She didn't have a single inkling and here he was, sweating and losing his shit. His brow dripped with the beads of sweat that resembled all the lies he had kept from his beloved.

If Silas were here, he'd be telling Astrid, "Pull yourself together, you feather-brain. She's your woman. Not your enemy!" But it was just Astrid alone with Isra right now.

He edged closer to her, his nose almost touching her face. Isra's eyes met his, softly digging into those brown hollow globes. She felt herself grow excited at what was hidden behind them as he watched her closely. He closed his eyes, reaching for her hand and intertwined his fingers between hers, clasping her hand inside his own with a firm hold. He pushed himself up against her chest before she could fight it off.

Astrid held her free hand above her head, affixing it to the wall.

He touched her lips with his tongue, licking them as he maneuvered into her mouth. He could taste rich strawberries on her tongue, reminding him of the lush countryside where they grew wild and free. Their red color dominated the fields in which he had grown up as a young hatchling.

He thought nothing more of the secret he held from her after that. Making love to her as the night sky shone a torch in their bedroom, brightening the dull dark walls, their two bodies merged as one.

ONYX the cat skulked around in the grass. The cat was barely noticeable as the moon provided little light to show his presence. His tail stood out as the shadows magnified it onto the dark gray walls to something three times its size. An owl hooted from a nearby tree but Onyx paid it no mind. He was glad to be out of the tower, managing to sneak away from Lady Isra several hours ago.

He prowled in the grass. An unsuspecting wild mouse peeked out from a crack underneath the tower walls. It was presumably out in the open, looking for food. Its body was raggedy thin and its fur greasy and wet. Winter was almost here so the tiny creature was scurrilously moving along looking for sources of nourishment.

Onyx didn't care much because he too was hungry. Being a house pet, he didn't get much in the way of tasty morsels. Astrid would often feed him scraps of meat but not much else. A mouse right in his midst was an opportunity far too good to turn down.

He positioned himself in the undergrowth. Quietly moving inch by inch, he launched himself at the terrified creature. Before the mouse had any idea of what was happening, Onyx swooped, lunging his claws into the mouse's tender flesh. Feeling satisfied, he ripped into the mouse, tearing off every piece of skin with his sharpened teeth. Enjoying every last bite, he sat noisily chewing at his food.

THE BLACKNESS of night swarmed around the tower. A blanket of stars was the only light amongst the dark cover. All was quiet in Shambre Fell. It was just after midnight.

If you were to look close, you would see there were hardly any clouds present, as if someone had sucked them up with a vacuum, vanquishing them from existence. In replace of them was a black vortex gathering around the tower of Lady Isra, ferociously dominating it. It hadn't been here earlier. It was newly planted. Something was brewing as the vast energy of the black fury made itself known to all who would take notice of it.

One would assume this was dark forces making their way into the home of Lady Isra, but Isra was a witch. She'd be able to fight it, whatever it was. She had powers beyond the imagination of most magically inclined beings as much as many would hate to admit it.

Lady Isra and Astrid had retired to sleep several hours earlier. Neither of them was aware of the dark energy that was lurking on the tips of their home. Even Onyx was fast asleep beside a rose bush, having grown tired after his delicious meal. His whiskers twitched in the cold air as he slept, loudly snoring.

Footsteps approached as a raven flew past the bright yellow moon. The footsteps softened until the raven was long gone. A figure completely in black stepped toward the tower, keen to make sure nobody was aware of their presence, checking out the glass window frames, ensuring no lights were lit.

Onyx stirred as the figure walked past him. He licked his whiskers upon waking, still feeling like he was in a dream state. Onyx's eyes lit up as the figure revealed their mass of dark blonde hair on their head. The cloak lifted away from their face showing those well-known features that confirmed to Onyx that this was the one he knew. It was Ronald O'Kutte.

It can't be him, Onyx thought. *Oh, my goodness, it is! My dear, sweet young one.*

Ronald quietly explored the terrain, being careful not to make a sound, for he did not want to be discovered creeping around here in the night. He was being cautious as Lady Isra was someone he had been acquainted with, yes, but he wasn't making the cause of his mission here tonight known.

Rushing from underneath the rose bush, Onyx stretched out on his hind legs toward Ronald. He wanted to approach this endearing person he knew so well. Knowing that Ronald might well be alarmed at seeing Onyx in this manner, he rubbed himself around Ronald's legs, looking eagerly at Ronald. He so wanted to be acknowledged by the warrior he was proud of but couldn't emit the words from his mouth to say so.

"Shoo!" Ronald called out. Clearly this individual didn't like cats.

Onyx backed away, his swishing tail in the air indicating his upset. He didn't understand why he would be rejected in such a manner. He felt tears coming down from his face. His eye ducts watered as he tried so relentlessly to get close to Ronald again. Emotions were prominent in him, but he couldn't express them as a cat.

But what was this strange behavior for a cat? Silas had observed that something wasn't right within the little cat, but nobody else had really suspected anything surrounding Onyx and how he had come to be there. He had been presented to Lady Isra by Astrid as a kitten and as far as anyone in the dwelling knew, there was nothing particularly special about him. Just a cat with a lot of feelings, ideals on how his world should be.

Onyx stared at Ronald, bewildered as he was heading straight for the ornate door into the tower. "Oh, my goodness, what are you thinking about trying to get in there? Please turn away. Turn back!" Onyx called out, only to be disappointed when he realized Ronald couldn't hear a single word he had said.

Ronald stared at the door. The antique look of it reminded him of a place he had once known. Closing his eyes, he took a deep breath. Touching it with his fingers and feeling the wood underneath his hard worn skin, for a moment, he looked like he might try to open it, but something inside him thought better of it. If there was a time to get in, now wasn't it.

There would be better ways to get to Isra. Isra was wicked in her heart and mind. But her heart had been touched by another. There would be a way to get in and hurt her, although Ronald wasn't sure how.

Ronald caught sight of Onyx. That black cat stared at him with a fascination he could not explain. The thick black fur stood on end as if the cat had been electrocuted. The warrior man could not understand why the cat was looking at him in such an endearing manner. He did not know the cat personally, nor did he care much for it. To him, it was just an annoyance animated in fur.

Ronald sniggered at the cat. The cat didn't say anything back. Ronald smiled wickedly. A sudden knowing came to him in a moment's pause. *Aha,* he mused. *I know now. I know just how to get to that wretched old witch, finally!* He laughed, looking at Onyx once more with a snide smile.

ISRA AWOKE STARTLED. A sound was coming from outside. Feeling it was just a bird chirping she ignored it, leaning back once more against Astrid's bare chest. Her shimmery white unkempt hair was splayed across his shoulders. His arms were wrapped around hers. Both of their bodies were mushed together, tangled up in white linen sheets. The window was open just a little to let the warm morning air in.

It was the first time in a long while they had spent a proper night together, giving into their passions in the early hours of the night. They were alone in their domain after what seemed like forever. Astrid had given in to his hunger for Isra as she had for him. He felt bad as he was keeping things from her. How silly of him. If he had been Silas, he would have known Isra was doing the same. Before they knew what was happening, Astrid had Isra pinned up against the wall with his head knee-deep between her legs. She'd screamed out in hysteria as he made his wanting of her known. And then all went silent.

Now it was the morning. Blue peeked out from the skies. The sun hadn't yet made his appearance. Isra had awoken in Astrid's arms.

She felt content in his presence. There was a sense of calm as they laid entwined in one another. Things had been chaotic for them both of late. He had been away. She had been distracted by the council amongst other things although she wasn't telling Astrid much about anything. That was unusual for her.

They hadn't had much time to be alone together since Isra had met Ronald. He wasn't sure why. Astrid knew there was no romantic connection between Isra and the mortal. She was just distracted by his arrival and things with Astrid had been strained ever since. Isra was still there to an extent, but her mind seemed to be elsewhere.

Astrid knew Isra had been off and wandering lately, curious at every little thing. He wondered if dark still lingered in her heart, watching her carefully as she placed an ear to his chest, smiling at every pitter-patter the bold organ made inside his body.

The raven turned man had often sent his brother Silas to follow her secretly on her morning walks. Sometimes she'd be sneaky and come out of the tower late at night when she knew Silas couldn't follow. Isra would sometimes toy with Astrid in the way that she knew he was prowling her but she'd tempt him just enough to get his masculine fire going. Astrid would also sometimes follow Isra, but it was baffling as he lived with her. They were united, but still he felt a need to keep tabs on his witch. The old nagging insecurity that she might stray from him was never far from the pits of his mind.

If Silas were here, he'd say, "Oh, you silly old fool. Can't you see she loves you? Get a grip on yourself, dear brother. Or better yet, reclaim your feathers. Stalking your woman, honestly!"

He paused, turning away from his beloved for a moment. Realizing so many hours had passed, he feared Isra might be catching on to his secret. She was none the wiser though. Astrid's fears of losing her were so deeply rooted inside his soul that all he could do was think the worst, imagining scenarios that hadn't even happened. He was wondering if she still felt as strongly for him since the day they'd met.

Astrid saw Isra pull the bedclothes away from her, sitting in an upright position and then climbing into a lace white dress. Her head was hidden for a moment as she wriggled into the delicate garment. He nuzzled her. Isra reciprocated his affection, placing a kiss on his left cheek. She turned to the doorway, proceeding to leave. All hopes of a long lie-in with his lover were dashed as she left the bedroom.

Astrid sat quietly for a few moments, pondering whether he should go ahead and start his day. Still completely stark naked with only a white sheet protecting his modesty, the raven-man considered the idea of dressing himself. He stretched himself out on the edge of the bed. His feet rested firmly on the floor. Suddenly, he heard a shrill scream come from outside. Quickly throwing on shirt and trousers, he dashed out of the bedroom, flying down the stone spindled staircase as fast as his feet could carry him.

"Arggggh! My poor baby boy!" came Isra's cry.

Astrid ran faster, recognizing Isra's voice. He got to the front door, almost smacking himself through it. He forced it open, staggering outside into the green mass of grass. He felt disoriented as he tried to focus. He felt dizzy. The world had been turned upside down on him. The brown, ornate, wooden door slammed behind Astrid. He could only stand motionless beside Isra, unable to comprehend the sight in front of him.

Onyx was dead on the ground and Isra was crying over his lifeless body. Her tears soaked his black matted fur.

"My poor beloved boy. Who could do such a thing?" she shrieked. Tears rolled down her pain-stricken face.

"I don't know, my love," was all Astrid could muster. He couldn't comfort Isra. He had no idea of what to say that would make this situation better. "I'm sorry. He was a strong one," Astrid said, wrapping an arm around Isra.

"No!" she shouted. She pulled away from him, pushing Astrid aside.

Isra turned her back to him, standing facing the gray pathway of which Onyx had been found perished. Astrid took three steps back, realizing that Isra was unreachable. Guilt built up inside his stomach as he realized this was all his fault. If only he had been honest with her. But no, he had secrets and hidden veils.

And now that Onyx was dead, he wasn't sure if Isra would forgive him if she knew the truth. All he could do was watch, grief stricken in the realization she didn't want him anywhere near her.

Isra looked to the skies as if they might provide some guidance. The heavens were about to open up. A group of gray clouds banded together in a cluster. She felt the cold wind of winter on her face. The sky filled and became heavy as if snow was about to tumble down.

Isra turned around, facing Astrid. "I have to go," she said, quiet in her voice. It was as though there was something she wasn't saying. Her voice showed fear and desperation. But she wasn't about to open up.

"Go? Go where?" Astrid asked. He reached for her hand, feeling her slipping from him. She was pulling away and there wasn't anything he could do. The raven-man felt powerless.

"I don't know," came her reply. She was solemn. Isra had never been like that with Astrid.

Astrid knew right there and then that she was gone. His Isra ran away from him in a flash, going toward whatever darkness was waiting for her amongst her grief. He didn't know how to react. He wasn't sure if he should run after her or stand by and allow her the time she needed to get past this, if she was ever going to get past this.

Isra was heartbroken about Onyx. Now that he was no more, Isra was inconsolable. There is nothing more painful in life than loving someone that is no longer able to love you. Isra knew this to be true.

With Onyx dead, all Isra had left was Astrid. There was Silas too who did his best to be a confidant for the witch; however, Isra favored solitude over company. That was the way she had always been, the lone wolf wreaking havoc in the dark of night, wandering the lonely path she had chosen for herself because she had felt that nobody in the world would walk it with her. And now she was running off to be alone once again.

Isra turned away from her raven counterpart, giving him only her silence. and strode down the pathway without a care of knowing where it would lead. Astrid could only watch in horror as his faithful beloved walked away from him.

14

___

Ronald O'Kutte was restless. He had tried relentlessly to get a decent night's slumber. It was apparent that was not happening for him on this night. He had been tossing and turning throughout the night. He still felt hyped up from the previous night.

Ronald had finally got revenge on Lady Isra. He had killed her cat Onyx, leaving him dead on the pathway for everyone to see. Only the warrior had done a number on the witch, befriending her and gaining her trust before murdering her precious black cat in the grounds of Shambre Fell while she slept.

If Ronald was honest, he would have wanted to take that raven-man Astrid away from Lady Isra, but with Astrid being a soul that was first and foremost rooted in the dark, the young man knew it was impossible, if not dangerous. Astrid was a man who would strike first, think second.

To summarize his victory, Ronald felt extremely proud of himself. He wasn't being modest. In his eyes, it was a life for a life. Isra had supposedly killed Ronald's brother Kane three years ago. The way Ronald saw it, killing helpless Onyx was justice deliciously served.

But he wasn't done yet. He still had grand plans for the witch. He just wasn't sure on how she would respond. Ronald had been indulging in the dark arts. Luring Isra deep in her mind where she would be powerless to resist Ronald's charms, he had an idea that it may be working as he sensed that Isra was slipping away from her counterpart Astrid. It was something Ronald took great pleasure in as he saw Astrid as an obstacle that would stop him from getting to Isra where it would hurt the most: her heart.

Ronald stopped his thoughts for a moment. It was almost midnight. Still feeling like sleep was his foe, he reached for his clothes on the chair beside him. Smiling, he buttoned his white-breasted shirt before pulling on a pair of maroon trousers just coming to the knees. Next, he grabbed his mighty sword, attaching it to his belt loop before pulling on his boots.

Standing idly by the doorway of his quaint cottage, he took note of his surroundings. Purple roses had outgrown their spot in the grounds below, stretching around the wooden door frame in a circular motion. Ronald wasn't much of a gardener so he would leave the roses to continue to climb around the cottage. *They aren't doing any harm,* he thought to himself.

It was getting chilly. Frost was glinting at him from the soft grass. Summer had gone as quickly as it had arrived. He remembered meeting Lady Isra back in the spring when the red roses in her gardens were blooming. The apple trees were brimming with their delicious fruits.

The frost told him that winter was almost here. Ronald knew the time was drawing near in which he would catch Lady Isra once and for all. He wanted the witch completely weak and defenseless. He knew there would only be one way to do that, to have her so desolate that she would turn her back on everything she knew and trusted, especially Astrid. This was Ronald's end goal.

Ronald stood silently at the doorway. He could see the mighty trees standing still had hardly any leaves left on their branches. A pile of red and orange leaves covered the ground, almost blanketing it. Very soon, snow would cover everything in sight.

Ronald wondered if going to the tower so soon after killing Onyx was a wise choice. He wasn't sure if he was ready to let her know who he really was just yet. Ronald had already established a relationship with Isra, but it wasn't enough for him. He yearned to know what frightened her out of her tightly formed skin. Ronald wanted to hurt Lady Isra.

He had spent many months cooking up an elaborate plan. He had been patient so far, engineering pleasant conversation here and there, but even he knew the nice little facade could never last. It would get evil sooner or later when he revealed his true identity and how much hate he had for her. Ronald knew there was a possibility his plans could come to a grand halt if Isra's counterpart Astrid got wind of any of it. Astrid wasn't like most men. He knew things beyond any mortal's comprehension as he had been surrounded with dark matter all his raven life.

Ronald was uneasy when he'd first met Isra's raven because he knew all too clearly that if Astrid became suspicious of any dealings Ronald had with Isra, his well-thought revenge could blow up in his face. There was another obstacle standing in his path. Lady Isra was not only a witch, but immortal as well, having sold her soul to darkness many years ago. Witches bound to darkness are not easy creatures to annihilate. It doesn't matter how many clever ideas one may possess. You can't defeat something that is impenetrable from harm ... or death.

Ronald considered this as he strode off into the night. He was feeling the chill in the air as he walked through the trees. He stopped as he came to a clearing in the woods. He hadn't come across this place before. A square-shaped piece of land filled with greenery and wildflowers. An archway was located in the middle of the green grass, a strong stone-built archway with a mirror inside it. The mirror glowed with radiating waves of energy moving up and down and in a horizontal fashion.

Ronald approached the archway's mirror centerpiece, reaching his hand out to touch it when suddenly he backed away. Startled by what he saw, he inched backwards.

A figure in a snowy white cloak stood on the other side of the mirror. Her face was completely hidden except for a waft of hair that snuck out of the cloak's hood. She was solemn as she stood staring at Ronald. Sadness could be seen in her although Ronald wasn't aware who it was hiding underneath that cloak. The woman pulled down her hood, revealing her white shimmery hair. It was Lady Isra! Her eyes glowed like lights in the cold, solemn night, her face streaked with bitter tears.

"Well, hello dear," she said. She wasn't smiling. "I thought I was alone," Isra confessed.

Ronald smiled at Isra. It was a first for him. A sly but sweet evil smile played on her lips, one that Isra was used to displaying. She felt like she was looking at a mirror image of herself.

"Sadly that is not s anymore!" he murmured.

"Indeed. I'm not one for conversation today, friend," Isra said quietly. She looked around her and then behind her, wondering if her words might be heard by some unknown foe.

"I'm sorry to hear of your troubles. Please do tell me what the matter is. Perhaps I can help," Ronald said.

Isra felt unnerved. Something was stirring. An element in Ronald's words caused her to step back further as she gathered her thoughts. She was trying to piece together all the information in a rational manner.

"It's no matter really. My cat Onyx was brutally killed on the grounds of my home sometime in the night," Isra explained. "I don't know who the murderer is, but I've felt at a loss ever since. He was only young. He barely had a chance to live a peaceful life."

Ronald looked at Isra, trying hard to contain his glee. He had Isra right where he wanted. He hadn't planned on the witch being so grief stricken. Her emotions were taking over as she fought hard to hold the black weary tears inside herself.

"Oh. I am sorry, dear," Ronald comforted, trying not to sound false as he sounded out the words. *Oh you're falling for my trap, hook line and sinker!* he thought. If he ever wanted a way to catch a witch, then this was it. Darkness was still in her heart. He knew that.

The real Isra is about to emerge at any moment, he thought to himself wickedly, *the true Lady Isra of the Dark who cruelly captured my brother and then vanquished him. Oh, I suppose because she fell in love that all the terrible things she did before went away! But wait; isn't the raven-man wicked too? Didn't the man named Astrid belittle and keep charge of my brother while under the witch's keep? Hmmmm.*

Ronald's erratic thoughts were silenced. Lady Isra was standing right by him. He should have known better than to think when a witch was right in his domain. He knew from years of hearsay in his village that witches can hear thoughts. So, he ought to be careful about what he allowed in his mind when one happened to be right by him.

Ronald watched Isra carefully. She said nothing, standing by him in complete silence. A vision in white, she was encased in the light. It was ironic as he thought her to be the black wearing type creature. Nevertheless, now was not a time to peruse over what one would wear.

Ronald was trying to decipher how he and Lady Isra were led to this spot at the exact time. Ronald was sure he hadn't cast a spell to manifest it although he had been studying the occult in a bid to hone in on it so that he may conquer Lady Isra by knowing her. But Ronald hadn't done this. Isra was wrecked with loss so she couldn't have done anything magickal. It had to be fate, but how peculiar she would land in his lap when he had only just been thinking of how to lure her to him.

He caught sight of something in the trees, taking his eyes off Isra for a moment as he was distracted. His thoughts went back to his original plan, coming to visit Lady Isra at Shambre Fell. Then he had been led by mystical influence, it seemed, to this clearing, one he had never come across despite knowing the forest like the back of his well-kept hand.

It was conspicuous that Lady Isra should be here right when he was. And to think he was going to call in on her at her tower. The consequences of that decision didn't even bear thinking about. It could have been dire for him.

"It's no consolation to your loss, but I've been restless most of the night," Ronald said.

Lady Isra managed a half smile. Curiosity lingered in her. She was befuddled with Ronald. How could one so wanting to get acquainted with the occult also be slightly leery of it? He also seemed anxious to be in her wake although there was something about him she couldn't get a handle on.

Isra had always pictured Ronald as a strong man, capable of handling any task that was thrown onto him. Here he was in the midst of the night, seeming worried that she was around but at the same time, Isra could sense a wistfulness about him, a sudden joy that was evaporating from him.

"Restlessness is a trait known to those that walk the night," she said.

"That it is," he agreed. "I tried to get a restful night's sleep but the night kept me awake. I am so glad it did, for the beauty in this forest is astounding," he said, gently picking up Isra's hand with his own and kissing it as he looked upon her.

His analogy of beauty was a compliment to her. How regaled he was that she would meet him in such a messy space in her own emotional breakdown. He felt lucky that she had come here so unexpectedly.

Isra was taken aback. She didn't know what to say. She lifted her hand away quickly so that Ronald fell to his side. He looked somewhat upset at the rebuke but maintained his composure. After all, he had other things in store. Keeping up the niceties was a must.

It wasn't that Isra didn't like his appreciation, but she was used to humans fearing her and not giving her endless amounts of gushing, falling over their feet for her. That she didn't like. You have to remember Lady Isra was a solitary soul. She wasn't fond of being the center of attention, although she was good at getting it when it sufficed to her needs. She much preferred to be alone. Having a mortal fawn over her like this was embarrassing to her.

Ronald then got down on his knees, a feeble attempt to win her over by way of bowing to her, but Isra shot a hand at him, signaling him to come back up to reality.

"Please don't do that. I'm not royalty," Isra said, firmly brushing him off.

Isra backed away a few steps. Her feet stood upon an uneven patch of grass made her unsteady. She made haste in balancing herself, taking her eyes off Ronald. Isra felt exposed, tucking her dress behind her as she regained her composure, safe in the knowledge she had prevented herself from tumbling over.

"Oh, I'm sorry." Ronald lowered his head apologetically in the realization he had likely offended her. "I had thought with the title 'Lady Isra' that you were a nobility of some kind. A sorceress that is so legendary that people feel the need to bow before you!" he said in a questioning manner.

He was dying to know all her deep, dark secrets. Ronald had quite the yearning for the fair-haired enchantress. He was entranced by her power and the beauty that resided in her, the slim figure that was cut so effortlessly. Even that elegant hair that shone brighter than the light of the moon fascinated him. Maybe he was even a little obsessed.

"No, dear. I just happen to be a witch. Let's not add anything fancy to it," Isra replied.

She didn't feel like getting into a discussion over how she had inherited the title and neither was she going to, although Ronald had noticed her lack of wanting to explain. And being a man that conquered things head on, fearless and prominent, he lunged straight in for the inquisition.

"Lady Isra, I can't help but feel that you aren't being honest with me or yourself for that matter. But it's of no disposition to me. Don't be ashamed. We all have secrets," he said with a sly grin.

Isra didn't respond. Her wide-eyed glance was enough to convince Ronald that he was getting to her. He could feel her breathing a little faster as she maintained her silence along with her polite stance. Ronald feared he was losing the interest of Isra. Her eyes drifted away from him. She was growing bored of this mundane man grilling her with a desire to know things that she didn't want him to know.

In turning back to her, he observed she was alone. He wanted to make that known. He didn't need any surprises so in Ronald's eyes, this situation couldn't be more perfect. Glancing across at her, he noted her eyes showed how emotional she was, standing here alone. The whites in her eyes were prominent; she had barely slept since the young Onyx's death.

"I don't see that handsome raven of yours for once," he said like he was trying to state a point that Isra was nearly always with Astrid.

"Astrid and I are having some alone time. I feel he doesn't feel as upset over Onyx as I am," she said.

She sounded upset, like the raven-man was cold and had no feeling to express as much as she had. Sure, Onyx was just a cat, but to Isra, he was like the child she had never obtained. Losing him was a sore wound inside her soul, one that already bore much grief from losses that she would rather regret.

Ronald saw this as his weapon. Any distance between Isra and Astrid, no matter how small, was perfect for his plans in luring her. The more alone she was, the easier she would be to reach. He smiled, piping up all of a sudden. "I must admit, it is nice meeting you tonight. I was hoping we could meet again," Ronald uttered happily.

The cautious look on his face told Isra he was being meticulously careful of how he said things. She could see that he was all too happy to be near her after hearing that things weren't going too well with Astrid.

"Well, I do say it has been intriguing, but I must go now," Isra said.

She was solemn again. Her cheeks were pale. She seemed cold in her movements. The wind gently breezed through her long white hair as she longed to turn away from all of it. She still found it hard to accept Onyx was gone. Astrid had abandoned her in a sense, in her feelings, anyway. She was alone in the world once again.

Isra had always thought she wouldn't miss those carefree days where she roamed the forest alone. Now she had proved herself right, for she didn't miss it. All she could see was vast green lands filled with misery and that deep sinking feeling that the magic was gone. The darkness was tripping inside her soul, begging her to let it out once more and for the first time since knowing the love of another, Lady Isra was tempted by the lure of the dark side.

Isra glanced upon Ronald as she turned around. She pulled the hood of her snowy white cloak up to her head, slowly as if she was enticing Ronald with some form of magic, a trance to lure him into her surreal world. She could have run away as swiftly as she could, but instead she engaged with him, accepting his need for attention, giving him more than he could handle as she revealed who she really was: a sorceress that spun the universe around her little finger, exacting things that young Ronald could only dream of.

If only she knew just how little control she had over that universe...

Not even Isra could see the ground slipping away from underneath her feet.

ASTRID RESTED on the gilded chair, sitting upright and his feet almost touching the floor. He was restless and fidgety as he couldn't relax. And while his arms were somewhat still, he felt the blood pulsing through his veins as he tried to gain control of his mind.

Lady Isra had still not come home from her late-night stroll. It was four o'clock in the morning. The sun would be rising in a few hours. Although Astrid knew this, he was worried as Isra didn't often stay away from him this late.

He tried focusing on the floor, on the red rug with gold spirals all round it. No. That didn't work. It just made him more anxious. The red reminded him of the blood that once stained Lady Isra's body as she laid motionless on a rainy night.

Astrid thought back to the moment when Isa had left him that afternoon, of how she had turned away from him, her hair blowing in the wind wistfully as she walked away. He allowed her to go although he felt like there was nothing he could have done to stop her. She was inconsolable. He couldn't reach her with any words of his choosing. Astrid personally felt like Ronald was responsible for Isra leaving. He didn't know for sure, but something inside him told him that the mortal wasn't completely innocent.

He hadn't liked Ronald from the moment he laid his raven eyes on him. Astrid felt he should have pecked Ronald's head off. He was so ticked off that the repulsive Ronald had been there looking at his witch, viewing Isra in all her vulnerability, all smiley with her as if they had been friends for centuries when the reality was he was just a stranger.

Ronald has got an agenda beyond what he proclaims, Astrid thought to himself.

He sat bolt upright as he comprehended the mortal's motives and what he wanted with Isra. Astrid's, Isra. Yes, she was his, so any man wanting anything with her was deemed morally wrong in Astrid's eyes. Astrid reminisced back to the day of the council meeting. Ronald was there all quiet, right until the end when he had introduced himself to Isra as he stood on her grand staircase.

Why Ronald was so keen to speak to Isra was bugging Astrid. He was so charismatic about it. He even flirted with her a little which irritated Astrid a great deal and worse, Isra was receptive to it. Maybe she was under a spell, but surely he'd have sensed if she was. He knew Isra well enough to know when something wasn't right with her and if witchery was involved, he'd smell it out.

Astrid knew he shouldn't think anything of the interaction with Isra and Ronald. Isra was loyal to him, he knew that. He paused in his train of thought. It was just him and Silas alone in the grand throne room, the very room that Isra fondly called the living space for she would spend most of her time frequenting by the window ledge, looking out upon the land. And when she wasn't staring at the world below, she'd be sitting in the gold gilded chair as Astrid was now in this moment.

He had only just begun to notice how quiet and still it was without Isra. His eyes turned to the fellow on the chair's jeweled arm.

The black feathers stood out in a silhouette as Silas sat silently, perched on the end, not moving so he could have been easily mistaken for a statue. Then in a nanosecond, Silas's bold, yellow eyes glanced at the window frame as a noise in the grass caught his attention before he turned his attention back to doing absolutely nothing.

Astrid observed Silas's brief stirring. He smiled to himself, looking at Silas but not saying a word. There wasn't any verbal communication needed between the two of them. Looks were enough for the brothers to assimilate what they needed to say. Silas was the brother that would scold and lecture while Astrid was the one who was more relaxed while also keeping balance in every aspect of his life.

When they were young hatchlings, their mother had always said that Astrid would be the trouble-maker and Silas would be the responsible one. As it turned out, Silas was the father figure, dragging Astrid back from the brink of destruction, speaking reality back into him.

As for Astrid, he felt he didn't need a father figure. He was quite capable of doing what he pleased without a hierarchy to boss him around. Astrid had never taken the time to ask his mother or Silas what his father was like. It didn't bother him.

Silas was the one Astrid looked up to, especially when his mother passed away a couple of years after Astrid and Silas hatched. Astrid respected Silas. He enjoyed having his brother around. It was true Silas was a little hard on Astrid, but he had good intentions, a trait that wasn't often seen by Astrid. When Astrid was back home, he was always on his guard. Always suspecting the worst in the humans that dwelled amongst the places he had learned to call home. He had become accustomed to moving around from place to place, flying away whenever his welcome had wavered.

"Is there anything you don't notice?" Astrid asked. A quizzical grin was plastered across his face.

Silas paused as he studied Astrid's grin, feeling the question was sarcastic. "Hmmm. For an old bird, I have quite good ears. I could catch hold of anything as long as it makes a sound," Silas replied.

Silas turned his attention back to Astrid. The rugged yet handsome raven-man was fading a little. His skin was pale from worrying over Isra's disappearance and he sat anxiously in his seat. His hands gripped the sides of the chair, sinking his nails into it. His feet barely touched the floor as he couldn't relax, breathing heavy in anticipation as he awaited his Isra to return.

Astrid kept faithfully looking at the door, hoping she would come flying though it at any moment. That image kept on playing over and over in his mind while Silas did little to counsel his brother. The older raven felt that it was pointless. All he could do was try to reassure Astrid with words of wisdom, but Silas felt even that was fruitless. All it would accomplish was make Astrid more anxious. The raven-man was unable to listen to reason in times when he was filled with dread.

And it wasn't just Isra going missing that was distracting him. Astrid had been like this before her disappearance, lying to Isra and Silas and creeping about in the dark of night whilst looking over his shoulder. Perhaps he was expecting something to implode in his midst.

Why Astrid was so unnerved was not clear to Silas. Astrid shared his life with a woman he was absolutely enchanted with and yet something was stirring within him. Astrid had lied incessantly to Isra recently. And despite the fact, he wasn't betraying the witch with another lover. Something was amiss with him.

Silas knew Astrid had been dishonest about some things, but Silas wasn't the type to unravel others' deceit. He sat unknowing, but his eyes were open and there was nothing he didn't see. Just lately, Astrid would wait until Isra was alone, then he'd stand silently watching her in the dark of night and just as those piercing green eyes were about to catch him, he'd turn away.

Silas felt it was odd how Astrid felt it necessary to prowl Isra when he was bound to her, but still something inside the raven-man had become rather off balance in the past few months. Silas wasn't aware of what it was. He had noticed a significant change in his brother, and he wasn't sure if it was for the good of his soul, or whether Astrid was undertaking a much darker path.

Astrid had been known to tread water in the darker side of life before adulthood. Silas believed that Astrid was possibly heading back down that road, but he didn't know for certain. Silas watched his brother carefully, not taking his eyes off him.

Astrid walked over to the window, looking out across the horizon. The land seemed so desolate and bleak. He had often looked out upon this elaborate view, but he had never seen it look so torrid. It looked like a mass of gray now, as if the magic was evaporating because Isra wasn't here.

"She's still not here, huh?" Silas called out.

"No," Astrid said.

Astrid leaned out of the window, longing to catch a glimpse of Isra amongst the trees. He presumed that Isra was staying out so late in an effort to calm herself before she returned to him. Maybe she was staying away from him until she was in a more balanced state of mind.

The night sky was darkened in a shroud of black and blemished with hints of navy blue in between the fluffy clouds. Astrid peeked at the moon, a motionless white circle, only just visible in the sky. It was fading away slowly with time, dissipating into nothing, just like his Isra had in his perception.

Astrid imagined Isra walking by at any moment, her long black cloak trailing behind her as she strolled toward the tower. Astrid wondered where Isra was. Was she asleep beneath a tree? Was she lying dead on the path in which she had set off on? He couldn't hush his busy mind. It brewed with thoughts of Isra's whereabouts and whether she would return to him the same person she was.

It was a strange thing for him to be thinking when he knew Isra would always be whom he knew her to be, the one he had fallen helplessly in love with. Although as ludicrous as it sounded, Astrid was feeling that the Isra he knew may not return to him. How such darkened thoughts had surfaced in him, he did not know.

15

Lady Isra was sleeping soundly as she lay against a robust elm tree. Comatose and unable to hear the sounds around her, her body was paralyzed as she laid in a deep sleep. Her eyelids gently flickered as images soared inside her imagination.

In the dark of night, Isra stood in the middle of a scene. All she could see was black. A veil of it covered everything in the black matter. She couldn't see anything. Light started to shine down as she realized there was a moon above her. From the moon's light, Isra could make out a tree in the midst of the twilight. Tall branches reached all the way up, making Isra feel so small as she stared at its trunk. She felt like a midget in its wake.

Isra felt something behind her. She turned her head to find green sparks floating above her, lime green, bright shiny sparkles, shimmering and buzzing around her ears. Slowly the buzzing increased as she found it barely audible to hear anything else. The green sparkles spun so fast, before Isra knew what was happening, they were spiraling into a vortex right in front of her, gathering speed as they grew stronger. Now Isra was unable to see anything else. Her eyes were drawn to the sparkly vortex as it glowed, almost blinding her.

She squinted in her dream-like state trying to force her eyelids open but to no avail. The green sparkles began whispering. They were calling to her. What they were saying, she did not know. The messages were garbled. She tried to listen but all she got was sounds. No words.

"Eeeeeeeee," they said over and over again. It kept on repeating.

Isra couldn't understand these creatures' language. It was like something from another world. Was she in another dimension beyond even her immortal knowledge?

"I don't understand you," she whispered.

The high-pitched noises forced Isra to smash her hands to her eyes, willing herself to wake. Desperate and anxious, she rubbed her hands into her eyes, keeping it up in the hope she would awaken back in her own land. She wasn't even sure if this was a dream, but as a sweet song echoed from the tree, she was rescued from her nightmare.

HER EYES OPENED AT ONCE, bringing everything in her world to life. She was groggy. Her body felt limp and heavy, perhaps from sleep as she had slept against a large elm tree.

Isra felt warmth on her skin as she felt golden sunshine shimmer down onto her face. Shifting from against the elm tree, Isra turned to her side, looking across to examine the scene around her. She was in a clearing in the middle of the forest. As she looked down, she saw her white cloak was slung across her shoulders, revealing her uncovered chest. Isra pulled it up to her neck.

As she stretched slightly, she presumed she must have fallen asleep in the dead of night. Isra had no idea of why she was here and not home. She had no memory of the previous night's events, except that ... Ronald! Yes, she'd encountered Ronald just before dawn, but why that was so fuzzy, she didn't know. It was as if her mind had been wiped clean so nothing could be gained from it. All knowledge of the rendezvous with the treacherous mortal, gone in a flash.

After her encounter with Ronald, she had felt quite drained. She knew that for certain. It was why she had left shortly after his interrogation of her. She had announced her departure to the mortal but after that, things had become rather hazy.

Isra tried her hardest to tune into nature's wonder as she fought to claim her memories back. She closed her eyes and allowed herself to drift off, not in a sleep, but in a meditative state. At first there was nothing, just a blank slate in her mind but she quickly countered this, whispering some choice words.

Ah yes, that was it. She had left Astrid and then had bumped into Ronald. He had asked her why she had the title, "Lady Isra of the Dark." She hadn't told him why and had shrugged off his lewd questioning. Then she had left him. But what after that? That was the part she was unable to retrieve from her mind.

Never mind, it doesn't matter, she thought to herself. *Time to get home. Astrid will be waiting.*

Isra stood. The sun glared at her, almost blinding her vision as she struggled to see through its golden mass. She peered from behind the tree. It was just her and nature, convening as one. She looked through a stray tree branch, staying at a safe distance as she checked the area. When she realized she was alone, she stepped forward.

A bright blue butterfly floated down onto her hand. Its wings shimmered with hues of turquoise and cream. As it glowed in the light, it looked like silver. The butterfly fluttered about for a few moments before landing on Isra's shoulder. She smiled at it as it flew away.

Edging forward, she stopped, staring at an open space. A bright yellow glow caught her eye, a serene area in a big square screaming with wonder and enchantment. She couldn't see what was inside the square as there was a wooden bridge standing in her view, but whatever it was, it looked so magickal.

Mesmerized by its charm, she was curious. She stepped closer to the bridge, feeling the cool breeze on her skin. She pulled her snowy white cloak around her tighter. Now that she was walking along the side, she stopped to admire it. It was made entirely out of wood, eloquently made by fine hands that had cleverly assembled it. Gray stone bricks were there underneath the wood. The rest was made of stone. Underneath the bridge was the stream Isra knew that led to Shambre Fell. Beautiful waters in soft cerulean blue gently flowed down to, Isra assumed, Shambre Fell.

Why she had never seen this place after all the years of knowing Shambre Fell, she wasn't sure. It had surely captured her imagination. She walked slowly along the bridge. Golden swans were swimming in the cerulean blue stream below the bridge. She had never seen such a graceful creature before. These majestic animals silently floated in the water. Isra couldn't help but admire them.

Isra crossed the bridge, noticing orange lanterns projecting a warm glow. Their warm shades reflected onto the water as she found herself closer and closer to the yellow squared place that had lured her this far. Her breath stilled as she got closer, knowing that the golden world wasn't far away.

Isra began walking into the golden lit wonderland. She found it wasn't a yellow mass, glowing like a candle as she had expected. It was a golden field with flowers and trees unlike any she had known before. Flowers covered the yellowing field brightening it in their bold shades of red and violet. A darker mood was portrayed as blackthorn trees stood all around with powder blueberries attached to emerald green leaves.

Isra walked to the center of the field. A simple rose all alone with no neighboring flora or fungi to accompany it caught her attention, a single black rose with purple thorns stood out amongst hundreds of red and purple roses. She had heard of black roses in her time, but alas, had never seen one although she had recollection of asking someone to seek one out for her.

Isra was curious so she moved closer to it. The rose was a pure jet black. The petals resemble themselves as fine silk. Dark red specks saturated the otherwise black rose, spotting it. The center of the rose was dark at night. No color could be seen from within it. Pure blackness.

Yet there was an alluring vibe emitting from this black rose. Isra felt deeply connected to it. She bent down to touch it, feeling its soft, silky petals as she admired its fragile purple thorns sticking out like spearing needles. One of them pricked into her skin as she touched it. Blood poured out from her index finger onto the black rose, cascading down onto the stem and the earth. Isra looked upon her blood as cleansing the earth although she wasn't entirely sure where that notion stemmed from. She wasn't feeling it was one of her own thoughts.

Something had captured her mind as thoughts began circling around inside her head. Her piercing green eyes were focused on the red liquid mixing in with the dark brown soil, tingeing it a maroon color as she found herself looking at the rose once more, fixated with it. The magic of this supernatural flower captured Isra as she was enchanted by it so swiftly.

She reached down into the earth, gently lifting the soil before lifting the rose out of the ground. Holding it in her hand, she brought it up to her face. Isra gently sniffed the rose's soft, sweet fragrance, taking it in. Her eyes were closed. She stood quiet, not a soul knew she was here. The scenery looked poignant. Isra stood in the middle of the field clasping the beautiful black rose in her hand.

All of a sudden, the world around her grew small. The golden field became distorted in her vision, twisting and swaying. It danced around her causing her to feel unsteady on her feet. The colors faded in front of her eyes. She looked at the black rose, still in her hand. Gazing at it, it appeared blurry to her as she looked upon it.

In a hazy moment, she tried to gain some footing to resist this magical enchantment. Attempting to stand up, she clasped the rose in one hand, using the other to dig her nails into the soil to anchor herself into the ground. She held on, clawing at the earth, trying with force to withstand the spell that was overtaking her with its mighty power.

On the brink of collapse and unable to hold on any longer, Isra fell to the ground with a thud.

16

Isra awakened with a jolt. Her eyes burst open as flashes burst around her. Her head was throbbing. Painful sensations ran across her forehead. She tried to justify where she was, then all of a sudden, she looked downward.

There she stood, standing above her own body. Lifeless, lying so poignant and still in the morning light. Her face was pale, complimenting the black rose still held in her cold hand.

It can't be, she thought. *Am I dead? No, this can't be so. If I perished, why am I still here? Oh, I need to find Astrid. Yes, Astrid. But where am I?*

Isra looked down upon her carcass, the same body that had allowed her escapade from its immortal skin. The snow-white cloak just about covered her small frame, hiding a long black dress that stuck out from beneath the white cloak's hem.

Isra looked closer. Open mouthed, she gasped. She saw her own chest rise and fall. That lifeless body looking so absolute as it laid in the center of the field was breathing in the spot Isra had found the black rose and succumbed to its deadly scent. She tried to fathom how her body could be living and breathing while here she was in the ethereal form, looking like just how she was before she had fallen, still in her snowy white cloak covering her slender form contrasting marvelously in monochrome as it delighted her black dress.

Isra was puzzled and fighting to unravel the puzzle. "Okay, I must be dead. That can be the only way to explain the inconceivable notion. But how can I be when my earthly form is breathing? Oh, this makes no sense! I just need to find Astrid, maybe he can fathom this tricky mess," she shrieked.

In her heady panic, she quickly realized she was alone and the only one that could hear herself. Nobody else would be able to hear her.

"I have to get to Astrid at once!" she said.

Stuck in her metaphysical form, Isra assumed the best way to find Astrid would be to first get moving herself, just like she would when she was in her physical form. Isra pushed her left foot forward, and then placed her right one beside it. With both feet firmly pressed together in the pursuit to stride, Isra pushed herself to walk, willing her spiritual form to move as she enacted the movement by way of thought. She took one step and then another.

"Okay, maybe I can do this," she whispered to herself quietly.

Isra took a third step, pushing her chest forward as if she was masking some form of confidence. In all her years as a dark witch, never had she had to falsify a feeling of bravery when entering the unknown because she knew it all. She had known she was mighty and fierce and nothing could stand in her way, however now that had all changed. She was treading water into a cold world where she was no longer in charge.

Lady Isra of the Dark was not victorious, for now she was the one under a spell. How ironic when not so many moons ago she was the one enacting terror and placing fear in the wake of anyone who crossed her. Instead, she was now receiving it, forced to relive her past deeds as now she could feel firsthand what that is really like.

Isra had never been cursed nor had she fallen victim to any spells in her life until this point. It was hard to imagine herself in this position. She had never considered herself a victim, not even in her teenage years where her heart had been turned to stone.

Isra looked up to see gray smoke swirling in front of her like a mist. It grew with rapid force as it became stronger, a cloudy, thick mist with tones of misery. Nothing could be seen in all this gray. No one would be able to tell if the land had disappeared or if it was just hidden by the mist surrounding everything. A chill came cruising through the smoke. The wind was blowing through the thin lace of Isra's dress, the coolness pooling at her feet as she felt it all over her body.

Isra turned around, pulling her cloak up to her neck in a dire attempt for warmth. Her eyes narrowed as they tried to perceive something in the distance. A gray, dense shadow began to form in the center of the vast cloudy gray covering. It was moving slowly toward her, a tall gray figure that closely resembled a thin tree. The shadowy soul was just about visible as it blended in with the rest of the misty haze.

As it came closer, Isra could just about see it was a person, however she didn't know who. The facial features weren't clear enough until the shadow fully came forward, standing opposite Isra. They were dressed in a long black cloak made of soft velvet, flowing to the ground. Their hair and face were mostly hidden by the cloak's hood which Isra found amusing despite the deathly predicament she was in.

Isra was unable to identify who they were, although for some peculiar reason she did not understand, Isra felt warmth from them. It was emitting from their souls like warm coals on a hearth, blazing from those eyes that were blue yet cold as ice. That told Isra it could only be one person. The very same person, she didn't expect to see ever again.

Everilda.

Oh, it can't be true. It just can't be true, Isra thought, bemused at such a thing happening in her wake.

Everilda lifted her hood, revealing her soft face. She smiled at Isra. She stopped in a pause, she was welcoming and warm. Isra's mouth fell open. She couldn't conceive of it. Staring back at her was her former friend and foe. Everilda stood waiting for Isra to speak, her glossy golden hair standing out amongst all the black.

"Nice to see you, dear," Everilda said finally, half snorting in amusement.

"I should have known!" Isra mouthed, taken aback that Everilda would show up now of all times.

"Sorry to disappoint you, dear. I have been dead for a while and as much as I'd love to see me and you fighting over who gets the hellfire, I'd rather do this," Everilda retorted, seeming annoyed that Isra wasn't taking her seriously.

"Evie. We'd never fight over the hellfire. We'd rule over it together," Isra joked. She seemed to have found some humor in the situation between her and Everilda as her mind slipped back to brighter times, days when she and Everilda would be laid out on grassy banks outstretched, talking about how they would someday rule the world with their combined power. Of course, dear old Evie never made it that far, but it made Isra smile, as much as she didn't care to admit it.

Everilda stared at Isra, curious to know if Isra was joking or whether she was serious. She half imagined her and Isra together in the afterlife although it seemed silly as they had much hate harbored between them.

"Yes, well I am dead. You are not. Yet," Everilda said gruffly. Her tone was soft but chalk-like in manner.

"No, I am not," Isra agreed. "But I'm dying to know why you'd be here out of all those I have known and vanquished."

Everilda tried not to laugh at Isra's mention of dying for she feared her former foe wasn't far away from it. Both witches stared blindly at each other. Their mouths were pursed as if to spit out something terribly crucial to the moment, but neither did so. The silence between them grew with unspeakable force before finally Everilda broke the mold.

"Because I'm the one you loved and hated the most," she said.

Isra's eyes narrowed at Everilda, their green glint darting

everywhere as she did her utmost to suss Everilda out. Calmly, she said nothing, only listened as the witch began to recall her torrid tale.

"I've heard you many nights, calling me out with that name, Everilda, the failure of all things. It hurt me at first, but now I realize you were right. I did some unmentionable things to you but more so to myself."

"That I agree with," Isra said pointedly. "Then there's the girl, Contessia. Trying to infiltrate my home with your spy, Klinq. And of course, Jonathan," Isra added.

A bitter taste roamed inside her mouth at just the mention of that sordid man's name. Jonathan. A disgusting specimen that she found even more repulsive since she had fallen head over heels for him, once upon a time. Everilda didn't disagree. Her gaze focused on Isra's solemn face, wondering if Isra did indeed agree with her notion while her friend was so drenched in the foray of their past.

"Well, yes, I agree. Anyway, that's not why I'm here!" she piped up.

"Oh?" Isra's ears rose as if she was awaiting a revelation coming from the darkest pits of Hell. Her eyes froze upon Everilda's face.

"The raven-man, as preposterous as I find him, does he know?" Everilda inquired. Everilda was serious, her face sobering and refusing to shift. The skin beneath her eyes was drawn out and saggy. Her skin protruded out at the sides of her face. Death had weathered her although one would still think she was the tender age of seventeen she had always been if you looked close enough into, dare I say, her soul.

"Astrid?" Isra asked.

"Yes. That bird you turned into a man. As much as I hate him, he's your salvation in this dreary circumstance," Everilda retorted, blunt as ever.

"Ah." Isra looked around baffled.

She still hadn't managed to find Astrid. Everilda's arrival had distracted her from her thought of finding him. She wondered where Astrid might be. Maybe at the tower wondering where she was or perhaps he had sent Silas out looking for her? She had not seen the fine fellow but there was a distinct possibility.

Isra looked around the gray clouds that surrounded her. Although Isra couldn't see past them and had no knowledge of whether it was day or night, she presumed many hours had passed. She felt night would soon be arriving. As she watched Everilda standing back in the shadows, Isra thought about Astrid again and how he would be worried, for she was still not by his side.

Isra's focus turned away from the clouds. She didn't notice a black mist gathering around her. She was too busy being fixated on Everilda, more importantly, why Everilda was here in this moment when Isra was close to the pitfalls of death. But Isra didn't need Everilda's help. No, she could take care of herself. Why would she need the assistance of a former witch who had managed to lose her powers anyway? The very idea was preposterous!

The black mist that had been gathering while Isra was concentrating on Everilda's involvement in this had now totally surrounded her. There was no chance of escaping it. The thick tar-like material fiercely saturated the landscape so nothing could be seen beyond it.

"Why would you be so precarious to know if Astrid was coming here?" Isra motioned to Everilda.

Everilda froze as if Isra had unleashed something she didn't want to face. A look of terror on her face was delicately hidden by the shadow of the black mist. "Because you've found the black rose. And I know what's coming next!" Everilda answered.

Her tone of voice seemed cryptic which seemed strange to Isra as she couldn't recall Everilda ever being mysterious or hidden in terms of her ways of articulating that which might be hidden.

"You sound like a prophet," Isra remarked. Her voice was filled with sarcasm. It was ironic she hadn't lost her sense of humour despite her predicament.

"Maybe I am one," Everilda retorted. She narrowed her eyes at the black pooling at Isra's feet. She stared at Isra as if she had been waiting for this for some time.

"Uh huh," was all Isra could say.

Black smoke rose up from her feet and dominated her entire body. It was swirling around her slender frame in circles, cascading upward, moving toward her head. She began to feel dizzy. It was strange, for she could not remain stable on the ground. Everything shook as the blackness took over.

She was just about managing to stay stood up when images flooded her mind. She couldn't make them out well. There was so many fluttering about over her head like little stars falling down from the heavens. If the images had slowed down a little, she might have been able to see them for what they were.

A man's face appeared in her view, desolate and lost as if he'd been searching for gold but instead found nothing but worthless coins. Golden waves of hair descended down to his neck. He was crying. The tears dripped down his face, soaking his cheeks. He was down on his knees leaning over a corpse.

Oh no, it can't be. Kane? Oh, my goodness, it is him. But wait, why am I seeing him? Isra thought wildly. The trance had taken full hold of her.

Isra watched as Kane bent over the lifeless body in front of him. The white dress of a woman covered in blood could barely be seen, it was so saturated. The blood was all over the poor woman's dress. Her peach face was somber as she slept eternally in the midst of it all. So peaceful. Almost like she had just been in a slumber and would soon awaken. Like Kane was her prince and he'd soon be kissing her back to life. But alas, this could never be. Isra quickly realized it was Lillian, the woman she had killed. But why was she seeing this?

Kane lifted his head up in the visual, turning toward Isra. He was walking toward her now, making his approach.

Oh golly, why is this happening? I'm being made to face it. To see what I've done and the impact it's had on her and him. But why would they care? They are dead, Isra said to herself, horrified at what was occurring in front of her eyes.

Kane stood before Isra, staring her in those piercing green eyes of hers. His hand moved to reach out and grab hers and before she could do anything to stop him, Kane grabbed her hand, pulling her forward. Held in his grip, he threw Isra forward in front of Lillian. Isra had to be careful to steady herself otherwise she could have fallen on top of Lillian.

Well, this was a novel way of punishment, she thought. Her eyes were up close and personal with Lillian's. Isra acknowledged how peaceful Lillian looked despite the brutal way in which she had been murdered.

Isra thought back to that moment. She had found it enriching at the time. Horrific as it was for Lillian, Isra had enjoyed enacting the killing. But if there was any need of reasoning to bring some kindness for Lillian and those who loved her, it wasn't a slow, drawn-out death. It was quick. Isra had told Lillian the truth about Kane and then had sliced across her chest with a dagger, cutting her and then swiftly removing her heart in one simple swoop.

To Isra's and Kane's amazement, Lillian's eyes opened in a flash, fluttering back and forth for a second as her eyelids regained their ability to open and close. It must have been strange since they had not done so for some time. Lillian moved her arms, feeling life in her hands. Her nails sank in the ground beneath the grassy mound she had been resting upon, clawing into the soil to give herself support. Slowly reaching upright, she stood herself up until she was face to face with the woman who had made her this way: Isra.

"You took my life away," Lillian squealed. "Why did you do such a terrible deed?" she asked, forcing a finger in Isra's direction.

"I don't know," was all Isra could muster.

Did she know? Isra had said at the time it was a suitable

punishment for Kane. In taking away the one thing he hadn't appreciated, she would make him understand just what it was to have lost it. This wasn't something you'd have expected from a witch, a dark witch shrouded in forces of evil, no less. How peculiar that one should be placed right next to their misdeed and suddenly not know why they committed it. Was Isra not sure of herself in this state? Plagued by what she had done, she could not see what was in front of her. How beguiling!

Kane said nothing, watching Lillian back away. She stepped backward, not looking where she was heading. At once, she was disintegrating into nothing, a residual entity shattering into dust. No less than a few seconds later, she was gone. There was no trace left of her. Only the memory would remain to prove she had once lived and breathed.

He hadn't even had the chance to say hello to her, let alone a goodbye. There were so many things he had wanted to express, to give her closure while seeking it himself. But life was a cruel being and so many times it had let him down, not giving him what he had wanted. He would have to accept that this was one of those times where he would have to go on. He would never know what Lillian thought of his betrayal or whether she had forgiven him. Such a sad thing to be weighing on his shoulders, but maybe someday they would meet again.

With Lillian gone, Isra was in Kane's view again, though he was not sure whether he was going to approach her. She stood quietly awaiting the worst. Whatever it was, she'd have to let it be, for there was no getting out of this vision-like state without getting what she deserved. And she suspected there was much more to come.

Kane glared at Isra. Seething anger showed the rage inside his eyes that were now blood red. He stared into her, digging into her view. Isra hadn't noticed them change, she had been so preoccupied with everything else and how she had ended up here.

He was bitter. Foul over his loss. She could hear the growling inside of him. Cries and shrieks he had uttered during the night only to never be heard; she could hear them all now. No longer were they silenced. The shrieks sounded inside her ears, pounding on her lobes. The pressure was overwhelming and she fought the urge to collapse. Her feet were unsteady once again. Hearing someone behind her or in front of her, she couldn't fathom it, completely unable to see anything. Her body was so weightless. The dizziness was growing.

Finally, Kane said, "I have been waiting for this day for a long time. Do you have anything to say, witch? Or was I just an entertaining fantasy for you?" he cajoled her.

She said nothing. Almost on the brink of collapse, she teetered between staying up right and falling down ... when suddenly, it was like she could hold on no longer.

He knew her time was coming to an end. She would sink at any moment now. The torture had been placed upon her in the most grotesque way it could have been delivered. Although he had not been able to see her truly suffer, he had said his piece but knew he wasn't going to get an answer, for she was so close to losing her grip on reality and the human world. He was dead, that was for certain, but he didn't wish to be on this earth any longer than he had to. A simple parting gift would be enough to suffice his needs.

Kane watched as Isra plummeted face down into the ground. Her dress splayed out around her, only just protecting her modesty. He reached down, touching her hair, stroking it. He had no emotion in his face as he ran his fingers through the white glossy ringlets, feeling every little last bit out.

Letting the time pass without worry that the raven would be here attacking him, Kane knew he could do anything to Isra and get away with it. He had no care in the world. He was relaxed, feeling freedom at last.

His fingers slipped through her hair like water. He lowered his lips to her ear and whispered, "I know you. I knew we would meet again and meet again when your zealous lover made me into your family pet."

Kane pushed Lady Isra's hair back across her ear. He looked at her for one last time. Her lips in the dull shade of crimson framed her face were a perfect mismatch to the paleness of her skin. As if frozen in time, she lies sleeping. And for all anyone knew, it was forever.

BACK IN A REALM where humans could not reside, all was peaceful in the heaven-like state where the winds were finally quiet. The sun was luminescent, hiding behind a group of shimmery white clouds. The light was breaking through as night had made its last goodbye, disappearing into another day.

In the distance, two figures stood in the middle of a grassy knoll splattered with the debris of gray bricks. Large pieces of ruin of what one would have presumed were a castle decorated the area. All that was left was chunks of what used to be.

The taller woman was dressed in a white cloak. Long ringlets of white hair poked out of the hood, spread out across the fur trim. She had a calm presence about her but her head turned sideways to examine the area closely as if she was watching out for something ... or someone. The other woman was dressed completely in black. She had a close resemblance to that of a widow as she was draped in black velvet from head to toe. A long jet-black cloak covered her agile frame while sky blue eyes peeped across the horizon, surveying the scene.

Both women seemed to be busy looking for something. It was strange as they were quiet and still but yet focused on what was going on around them. This was a beautiful place they were in, so full of light despite the broken bits of stone scattered all around them. These two had personal history. Perhaps a scenario in a former life where they had once been friends. They were distant but yet calm with each other. Neither looked like they wanted to speak for fear of rocking the boat but things would be said sooner or later, you would think. There would be no other reason why they had come together in the small hours of the dawn.

This had to be an auspicious meeting of minds and souls, one that would wreak havoc into old wounds and maybe create some new ones. The tension was almost as warm as the absent sun. You could feel the warmth but yet when you looked close, you couldn't tell if they were at war or about to lay down the swords at each other's feet. The woman in black named Everilda parted her lips, pursuing them mid pause. The other, Isra, looked back sullenly before turning away, clearly not in the mood for conversation.

"I'm sorry you had to find out this way," Everilda called out to Isra.

Isra turned her head to face Everilda. She'd had a rough few days, that was for sure, but was she broken? She didn't think so. There had been many aspects of life she'd had to face and the revelation from Kane that all was not as well in her world as it had made out to be was just one in a long line. In short, Isra was used to being betrayed, but Astrid? She couldn't quite believe it.

But she also knew a spirit, one that had left earth for the spiritual realm, could not lie. It was forbidden as only truth was allowed to remain from the midst of whatever human life the spirit had led prior to death. Everything else would be stripped away. Sweet, lighthearted beings ripped away the foundations built by love and loss, tearing down the karmic cycles and bringing them to a grand halt as it was no longer needed in such a divine place.

Isra knew that despite being surrounded by much darkness even she would meet her end one day. It doesn't matter how invincible you think you are, you are never really invulnerable to chaotic destruction. That had been solely proven to Isra by the predicament she was in now, being in an ethereal place which was an uncanny resemblance to Everilda's former home, except in this land the ruins had been brought along with Everilda. The heavenly plains weren't about to resurrect Everilda's grand palace in all its former glory.

Isra suspected it was like this because this was how she and Everilda had parted back on earth. She had been standing here and had summoned Everilda before telling her a few home truths. Everilda's old home was still intact by that point, but the standoff between Isra and Everilda had finished it off for good. And this was all that was left.

"Oh, you mean Astrid?" Isra laughed.

She seemed amused by the idea that Everilda was sorry to hear of Astrid's betrayal because the Everilda that Isra knew wasn't sorry about anything unless it was pertaining to her.

"Yes. I am truly sorry you had to find out that way," Everilda concurred.

"Don't be. I knew Astrid had set his sights on getting Kane out of our lives for good. He had said he would ensure that, but I didn't know he'd go this far to do so," Isra muttered.

She paused, waving a stray white ringlet away from her face. She looked up toward the sun shining above, gently in the distance.

"You know, I've done some sordid things in my tenure on this earth, but never in all my years did I expect to get a taste of my own medicine, to be so harshly reminded of what I had done. Yet there it was right in front of my face, glowering at me, the taste rancid like sour rain that had lingering for days but only just erupted from the skies. It was like a gross sensation of feeling something coming down on you but for the first time ever, knowing what it was really like to feel something so horrific and terrible that even you cannot understand your motives for it. I've taken lives, both animal and human," Isra continued.

Her breathing became slow, and she paced as if she was releasing a torrent of emotions. "But I never once thought of coming face to face with someone who I had truly hurt and that they in turn would hurt me. That was a new experience and one I never expected, but it just goes to show we can never really predict anything, Evie. That's the mystery behind life. It's always there waiting for us to trip up so it can show us who is really in control."

Isra smiled at Everilda, a small curt smile full of promise. It reminded her of a time when they had been on even grounds, of when things had been much simpler for them both.

"Well, I am shocked to know you finally found remorse, but does this change anything? For we both know you are a creature of the dark, Isra, as am I," Everilda retorted. A slight tinge of hilarity could be detected in her voice as if she didn't believe Isra was truly sorry.

"Good question, and I don't know. How can one know one's

future when it's so clouded with judgment of the past?" Isra questioned. She was referring to the past being that of her history with Kane and her behavior prior to her entering the dark world. Much blood had been split as she had got closer and closer to darkness. "I'd like it to be so, but I don't think there is a world big enough for me and you. We'd only end up destroying each other. Oh wait, we did that already, Evie. Oh, how I wish we could go back and resurrect those days, but the fact is we can't. We both sealed our fates," Isra finished.

Even if she could go back in time, back when she and Everilda were teenagers, she wondered what difference they could have made. They were so young back then and so naive. It only took a man to come between them, one small man who had ideas beyond their own, to have both witches fighting over him at his feet. If only he had known they were witches at the time. He could have saved himself a lot of trouble. However, he wasn't important in the matter. They had grown older and wiser and he was the last thing on either of their minds, or so Isra had assumed.

Everilda raised an eyebrow quizzically. She felt brave, opening her mouth and feeling like she was opening Pandora's Box, about to unleash something that should possibly stay locked away.

"Do you ever think of Jonathan?" Everilda asked, shooting the question at Isra's direction, not feeling sure of where this would lead them. A can of worms opened, one that could be launched at both of their faces, worms so rotten that all that would come from it was bitterness that was best buried.

Isra shrugged. She suddenly had both her arms close to her chest, folded in defense. "No, I don't but after what we both did to him, why would you care?"

"I don't," Everilda replied. "I just wondered if you ever thought of him?"

Isra's reply came swift. "Not really."

"Not once in all these years?" Everilda probed.

It was like she was trying to provoke something here, to stir something in Isra that had been buried, but maybe Everilda wasn't convinced that it had been for definite. A fair amount of prodding may well prove otherwise.

"No," Isra stated. "Well, I thought I wanted to kill him once. Anyway, why are we discussing this fool?" she said, changing the subject. It was apparent that Isra did not want to talk about Jonathan.

"No reason," Everilda replied. "I just thought since he was the reason we went our separate ways that perhaps underneath that sharp mouth and foul temper that maybe in some simpering way you still had some feeling for him still."

Isra threw Everilda a disgusted look. It was as though she had just stepped in something and needed to scrape it from her shoe. Nothing could disguise how repulsed she was by the very idea that she may still possess feelings for that.... that *mortal*.

Vile. It's simply intolerable. How putrid. What the hell goes through that warped woman's mind? Isra thought callously to herself in reference to Everilda. "You were always a strange creature, Evie!" Isra called out.

"Yes, as were you!" Everilda retorted back. "Killing a dragon to claim the power of the blackened? I mean really Isra, did you honestly think I wouldn't get to hear of that?"

Isra said nothing, blushing slightly. She stood with a cold look in her lime green eyes searching into the distance. Behind her and Everilda lie acres of greenery that had been here on the night Isra had confronted Everilda using love as her weapon. The love Isra had with Astrid. Isra had used that to vanquish Everilda once and for all. When you think of it, it was the ultimate force against Everilda as she had never learned to love another.

"How did you get to learn of such an event?" Isra pressed. Curiosity surged through her heart. It was interesting to Isra how Everilda, a mortal with no powers whatsoever, had managed to get wind of some of the darkest acts Isra had enacted. And she would have guessed it wasn't just because Klinq was Everilda's eyes and ears.

"Your dear friend, Romeo," Everilda commented. "He was a remarkable soul, right until the end."

Isra gasped. Poor Romeo. Sweet, caring Romeo. It broke her heart to think of him. She had hoped his death was without pain, but knowing Everilda, that was unlikely.

"Yes, Astrid told me about that, how Romeo had died at your hand," Isra explained.

"Well, I can't make up for that, but I had questioned him and when he had refused to tell me what I wanted to know, well, you know me..." Everilda trailed off.

It was evident she didn't want to elaborate just how she had killed Romeo. His murder was enough information for Isra. There was no point in opening up another wound when they were beginning to see things on the same page. Isra turned her head away from Everilda, not wanting to acknowledge her, like enough had been done.

"Yes, I understand. There's no need to rake over old coals."

Everilda looked at Isra, and for the first time in eons, she appeared happy. How ironic after years of the two of them being at war that they could finally come to some understanding and move on.

"Well, I guess my job here is done," Everilda announced. "I truly wish you well and should you ever need me for anything at all, just call my name. Even in the hearth of hellfire, I'll hear you," she said softly, moving backward until her spirit had totally vanished.

18

Contessia crept around the doorway as two male voices talked. Her long purple hair trailed behind her, some of it had snuck into her white dress from the nape of her neck. She stood keenly, her ear pressed to the space between the door and the wall trying to listen. She didn't want to be caught eavesdropping, however Isra was still not home. From what Contessia could gather, Astrid and Silas were talking but she could barely hear what they were saying.

Contessia didn't know why Isra was away, but she knew something was up. Astrid and Silas wouldn't have been whispering if there was no cause for alarm. Astrid barely said a word to Contessia on a good day, so she knew if she was going to find out what was going on, she'd have to be sneaky about it. She pressed herself in the doorway so that she was right in the corner. Her entire body pressed against the wall in a vain attempt to nose in on what Astrid was saying.

"She's been gone almost two days now," Astrid exhaled.

"Yes," Silas agreed, standing back and facing Astrid. Silas was the one who had a level head in this situation. He was calm, not panicked, waiting for Astrid to instruct him.

"Someone must know where she is," Astrid whispered, keeping a close eye on the door as he spoke.

He was keeping his voice as barely audible as possible for a reason. He didn't want that damn Wiccan girl messing anything else up. Things were bad enough with Isra missing. He didn't need any more drama in the household. Silas ventured forward, preening himself as he stretched out on the pile of books sat by the grand chair illuminating in its golden pristine color.

"Yes, but who?" Silas inquired.

Astrid said nothing for the moment, going back to the events before Isra had disappeared on him. She was upset because of Onyx's murder and prior to that, there was the council meeting that had ruffled her feathers quite a bit. Namely because Magnus Wingdom, Isra's former teacher, had ruled that the union between Isra and Astrid was too dangerous to exist. Naturally, Isra had ignored his concerns, showing him out but it had put stress on her.

However, she wouldn't have left due to that. No, there must be something else. Oh goodness, what could it be? Who in the very small circle they frequented would know where Isra was?

Let's see, Astrid thought, putting his finger to his lips. *Romeo is dead. Klinq that cowardly gnome has left after being banished, yet again. Contessia is in the tower although she wouldn't know anything anyhow as she hides in her bedchamber, away from society. Silas is here. Everilda is dead and rightly so. Onyx has sadly perished.*

Then it dawned on him. Onyx.

Oh, my goodness, he thought quickly. *That's it. It's Onyx.*

Astrid sank to the floor. His body was heavy from the guilt surging from inside the pit of his stomach. "It's all my fault," he cried. "I should have told her when I had the chance." He reached out his hand to the chair to stroke the feathers of his brother but Silas had flown off.

You see, Astrid had been keeping a ghastly secret from his partner, and not just any secret. It was something that she wouldn't even begin to imagine. It had begun when Isra had shown the slave boy Kane his dead bride, Lillian. She had told him he was free to go and he never showed up after that. Or that was what she had been led to believe.

Astrid sat on the floor reliving it. It seemed like only yesterday when he had caught the reckless Kane creeping around the grounds of Shambre Fell.

~

IT WAS THE EVENING, three days after Kane was let go. Astrid was lurking in the grounds, smelling the roses. He had never smelt such a divine fragrance. Now that distraction Kane was gone from his and Isra's lives, he was keen to celebrate the rest of his life with her. He wandered around, grazing from flower to flower, taking it all in.

Isra was no longer bound to revenge. She'd had her fun with the boy, Kane. Wickedness no longer resided in her heart and neither did she have a desire for it. She had accepted that as dark as she was, she could love and be loved. The most important part was that she had allowed Astrid into her heart.

Astrid wanted to plan for their grand future together. He was out there in the gardens for some quiet reflection. The sun was just going down and he was about to go back in through the grand ornate door when he heard rustling in the shrubs. He had assumed he was alone. Astrid slowly walked down the narrow path that led from the tower down towards the stream, making haste to keep quiet as he did so. The rustling stopped.

Aha! He smiled. *I've got you now, whoever you are, oh come out, come out! I won't bite.* Or perhaps he might, depending on who or what it was that was sneaking around his home.

Astrid ran through the grass. The blades touched his legs as he was only moments away from the stream. He stopped at once. His eyes locked into those of a perturbed, worried individual. He couldn't believe it. It was Kane, the slave boy, the one that had only just been let go of, a few days ago. At least he had changed his clothes, now dressed in a fashionable red shirt combined with sharp black trousers and shiny new, black boots.

Astrid turned to the boy and boomed, "What the hell are you doing here? Didn't you learn your lesson from before?"

Kane shrugged his shoulders, staring at the raven-man's bold eyes. "Something told me to come back. I shouldn't have, I know."

"Something, or someone?" Astrid questioned, his arms folded.

Kane straightened his glance. His eyes sparkled, like his passion for yearning all things magick had been renewed. But how so when his seeking out Isra had turned out to be so disastrous for him? "A lady witch. She claims to know Lady Isra," Kane said. His arms hung down by his sides. He looked foolish yet maintained eye contact with Astrid.

"What lady witch? There is only Isra," Astrid cajoled.

"She claims to be the very same," Kane uttered with confidence.

What lady witch? There is none. Astrid was getting irritated with this boy. Why hadn't he just left when he had the chance? Stupid man, looking for more. How very, very stupid. Isra would be furious if she knew about this. *Oh never mind, she won't have to,* Astrid thought.

The raven-man suddenly had a smile appear on his face. He wouldn't have to worry Isra, for he could take care of this without her knowing a thing. Astrid turned to Kane once more, his arms unfolded as he knew exactly how to deal with this "human," as Isra would call him. Astrid stood silently, thinking to himself. Kane had the nerve to just show up here without a care. Now he would reap the consequences of his weak choice.

"No, you're right. You shouldn't have, but it's no matter now," Astrid said.

Kane wasn't sure if he was about to be applauded or tossed into an open fire. He observed Astrid wasn't angry. He was as cool as it could be. This made Kane nervous. It didn't take long. After a few brief moments of staring between the two men, Astrid looked at Kane one last time.

And with that, Astrid clicked his fingers. He envisioned Kane in a blurry cloud of black, swirling around him as the magic got feistier. He spun around in this vortex of nothingness until finally in place of Kane, sat a little black cat.

If only Kane had run before Astrid had got to him.

Minutes later, Astrid presented the kitten to Isra. And that was how little Onyx had come to be.

Astrid's reverie came to a grand halt. Kane was their family pet, Onyx. Onyx had just been killed only a few nights ago.

"SHIT!" Astrid shouted.

Without stopping, he bounded out of the room. The door flew open, smacking Contessia on the head, feeling the wood on her skull.

"Owww!" she shrieked. She removed herself from the doorway, standing in Astrid's way.

"What the hell? That will teach you to eavesdrop on private conversations!" he barked solemnly. Astrid softened his stance, realizing it was his rushing out here that had caused this knock on her head. He reached his hand out to her, although she cowered away, backing toward the wall away from him. "Do not fear me. I've already done the worst I can to you!" he reminded her.

Astrid placed his hand across her forehead. It was a little warm. A slightly open slit on the side of her head was building up with heat and pressure but luckily there was no blood. This told Astrid she wasn't in any danger. Despite the jolt from the heavy wooden door, she would be okay.

"Have you seen my brother?" Astrid questioned her.

"No," Contessia said, quiet as a mouse. She was shocked that Astrid was being so warm toward her. Or perhaps he was just being charitable for he had caused the graze upon her head.

Could there be goodness in this man's heart or lack of one? she pondered to herself before swiftly shooting up the stairs so that he could not follow her. The sweet-tempered Contessia did not want to hang around to find out.

ASTRID LOOKED ON BEMUSED, but then discarded the thought. He had things to take care of. "Stupid girl is no use to me anyway!" he cursed to himself as he flew down the stone staircase. His feet bashed into every step. His energy conducted along with his fiery mood, crashing down onto the stone until he arrived at the bottom. "SILAS! Silas, where the hell are you?" Astrid shouted.

He launched himself into the ornate door, practically throwing himself at it. Looking around outside, thinking Silas might have gone in search of food, he charged through the grass blades, looking up at the tall apple tree. Those ripe, ruby red delectable fruits hung off the ends of the thin branches looking bold and dangerous.

Astrid thought for a moment about reaching up and grabbing one of the scrumptious fruits but then he thought better of it. Astrid suddenly had a recollection of the time when he and Isra had found themselves in an enchanted garden. It was the handiwork of Everilda although neither Isra nor Astrid wanted to admit it at the time. For one so limited to mortal ways, Everilda had managed to conjure up a lot of magic.

It had started one late summer afternoon only a year ago. Isra and Astrid had found themselves in a state of boredom, so both had opted to go for a walk. He chose to remain in his raven form so he could fly off at any moment, keeping his beady eye open for any of Everilda's tricks. Instead of going through the forest like they usually would, Isra had suggested a different route.

Soon enough, they found themselves in a surreal paradise with shimmering flowers in every color you could imagine. Fairies were found to be populating on the flowers as they went about their merry business. Then hidden away at the back of this place, Isra had found herself drawn to a very similar apple tree, just like this one. It appealed to her sense of whimsy and childhood curiosity. She reached out to touch it before pulling away her hand in the realization that it wasn't all it seemed to be.

It was then that Isra confirmed Astrid's feeling that something wasn't right in that place, thus prompting them to leave. How novel of Isra to insist they plant an apple tree in the grounds of Shambre Fell as a painful reminder of Everilda's failure to conquer her. Isra did love to gloat although this was symbolic as she knew the apple tree would be a sore bruise to Everilda's ego. Isra could be very creative in getting a specific message across when she thought hard enough. She painted a picture with such bold imagery that got right to the heart of what she wanted to say. Oh, how he missed her sharp, sarcastic mouth and dry humor.

"Plant the apple tree. I want apples as rosy, red as the look on Everilda's face," Isra had insisted, a cheeky look hiding under her crude smile.

"Yes, my love," he answered her, almost hysterical in response. It was safe to say that he got the joke.

How he wished Isra could be here now to make him burst into spontaneous laughter with her wit and warped sense of humor, but he had to find Silas first. Talking to his brother right now would do Astrid a lot of good. Silas would be able to help, he was sure of it.

Just as he was moving toward the taller green grass, Astrid spotted Silas on the ground, patting his feet on the bare earth, presumably hunting for tasty worms as he was digging his beak into the soil repeatedly. Bashing the earth and awaiting for something to surface, he suddenly poked his head up and noticed Astrid staring down at him.

Silas discarded a worm from his claw, realizing lunch was something he'd have to have later. The look on Astrid's face was enough to tell him that more serious matters were at hand, like a watercolor picture that was fading with time, murky and nonexistent. Astrid bent, kneeling on the grass. As if to get comfortable, he crossed his legs. He turned his head, darting his gaze back toward the tall tower behind him before looking away.

Astrid looked up at Silas as if just staring at the wise raven would provide some council. He'd done many things in his time as a raven, but none of them came close to the deeds he did as a man. A fully fledged and grown man that was capable of thinking up solutions to problems would always come up trumps to resolve the challenges that came upon him. However, this latest one made Astrid feel like he had plunged too far into the ocean. He wasn't sure on how to get back to the clearer, calmer waters.

Isra was gone, something he had never envisioned happening. Yes, she had died on him once already, miraculously brought back to life, but he didn't see this coming. It was ironic for someone who had spent most of his life seeing every moment before it came to be in the earthly realm.

A wise seer raven had once told Astrid, "You can't get a strong hold on life. You can't do much to control anything, however you can get a grip on how you react to the gifts it gives you. What one perceives as treacherous could actually be good. It's just all about our perception. How we see things makes them change for the better in our own way."

And he had kept those words with him ever since. He knew it was how you saw things that made them good or bad. Yes, some things in life were truly horrible and it was best to not go anywhere near them, but then some things would surprise you. Astrid knew that.

That had been true when he had first laid his eyes on Isra, back when she was seventeen. She sat weeping over a man who had torn her heart in two. Even then, he saw her for what she was, a powerful sorceress that, despite her rage and thundering boulders of anger, could do immense things. Astrid had waited for the right time to find her again. And find her he did years after that when she was in the throes of darkness. It didn't matter, Astrid's mind was already made up. He was going to get acquainted with her. He'd shined down his light into her blackened heart, seeking out the real Isra within.

Silas looked up at Astrid. He narrowed his eyes with a stern frown. "Oh, I cannot even begin to imagine what a mess you are in! Come on with you. Tell your brother all about it!" he chirped.

Astrid looked Silas dead in the eye, as if his raven brother was being far too light about this. He sensed a dash of sarcasm in Silas's words. "Don't patronize me. I know I messed up," Astrid chided.

"Yes, dear. You make messes look like avalanches on a good day. I feel you've really gone and done it this time, haven't you?" Silas said. A half smile formed on his face.

"I really wish you wouldn't reprimand me." Astrid sighed.

Silas dropped his head in disapproval. "You know, I really do envy you, Astrid. Here you are, so blessed to have someone who cares about you. A life with power, and amidst all of that, you choose to hide a deadly secret from the woman you claim to love!"

"I do love her!" Astrid declared.

He felt annoyed that Silas wasn't seeing his point of view. How could Silas know what this was like? He wasn't living in a human body with all these feelings. These torrid emotions made him wonder if he was going up or down. Being a raven was much easier to deal with, but he had made his choice. He was human now and he was going to have to live with it if he was going to come out of this alive and intact in his mind.

"And yet you keep secrets," Silas reminded him.

Once again Astrid felt the torture of his terrible mistake hammering down into his soul. He should have told Isra. *Yes, I should have.* Would she have understood if she had known Kane was their family cat? Would she have felt the same way feeding him scraps of meat and delicious tuna steaks if she had known the truth of how he came to be with her?

Never mind that, he thought to himself. *I need to find her first. Save her from that treacherous mortal and then worry about what she thinks of me.*

"Yes, I know, but instead of beating down on me, how about you help me?" Astrid shouted.

Astrid was angry, his fingers twitching as he tapped them furiously on the ground in a bid to control his raging anxiety. The blood pumped inside with every tap as his fingers pounded on the ground, louder each time. He found it hard to keep his temper when he felt the pressure building upside him. The anxiety of it all, the fear of someone discovering his secret before he had the chance to disclose it to Isra was too much. His queen. His warrior. The one he was so terrified of losing! He'd do anything to get her back to him.

That made him angry, but more angry at himself than anyone. He just couldn't bear it as too much was at stake. He didn't even know where to begin if he did reach in and tell Isra because there was so much that she didn't know about Astrid really.

Silas sighed, silently nodding his head. *Astrid will have to learn from his own mistakes,* he thought. *There's no purpose to me guiding him for he won't listen, but when has he ever listened to me? It was like this when we were young. He would go into the sunset, flying into the bold, fluffy clouds when the sun was at its strongest without fear when he knew he could be burned and still he did it, going against the advice of his elders when they knew what was best for him. How could it possibly be any different? He loves this witch, yes, I can see that. Anyone can, but he has to sort this situation out himself. If I guide him now, I fear he will continue to rely on me like he always has, thus never resolving his own problems.*

"All right, what's up?" Silas chirped.

"I have an idea of how to find Isra," Astrid mumbled.

"Oh, how so?" Silas queried warily, wondering what revelations were about to come out of his brother's mouth.

"A while back, Isra and I had a man trapped here in the basement. His name was Kane and he was our slave. He was let go after Isra delivered a fatal price to him. She befriended his bride-to-be, before shortly killing her," Astrid explained, needlessly rubbing his fingers together. The anxiety brimmed through him as he plundered on.

"Oh, my goodness, I knew she was dark, but that's a stretch too far," Silas interjected.

"Yes, well after that, the boy left, we thought that was the last of him, but what Isra doesn't know is..." Astrid's voice trailed off.

Silas staggered toward him, narrowing his eyes. He ruffled his feathers, stretching out. "Oh goodness, I dread to think what is coming next," Silas gasped.

Astrid reared his head toward the tower, looking up at the top window with its black iron frame. That tower is so instrumental in its own way. He had so cleverly hidden Isra from the rest of Shambre Fell in there.

"The boy came back," Astrid said finally. "I caught him and told him he shouldn't have been trespassing. I didn't like his motives so I transformed him into the cat that I presented to Isra."

Silas's beak dropped open in response. "Ah, so your little cat was not how he seemed to be. Now that you mention it, I found him to be quite strange as he spoke of being a warrior and I found it odd. He spoke so passionately about honor. I tried to advise him, but he was a peculiar little fellow," Silas reminisced.

"Yes, well there is more to this cautionary tale," Astrid admitted.

"There always is with you, Astrid," Silas cajoled.

"The council that used to school Isra arrived to see her. One of their guests of the love and light brigade as Isra refers to them was none other than Ronald O'Kutte, Kane's brother. He took an instant liking to Isra, much to my disgust. I was on her shoulder. I had to restrain myself from pecking that man's eyes out!" Astrid admitted.

Silas bent his head in disapproval. *I can see where this is heading,* he thought to himself. *I knew there was a reason he didn't like that mortal, but now we are finally getting to the truth of the matter. I just hope there can be a happy ending to this catastrophe.*

Silas disliked it when things couldn't be happy when it came to it. As a raven that had seen much loss and death, it was his preference to see people joyful. He was hoping this would be the case for Isra and Astrid. "And he doesn't know that cat was his dearly departed brother? Well, missing brother," Silas interrupted.

"No, Ronald doesn't know," Astrid muttered. "But I am sure he blames Isra for Kane's disappearance and he has every reason to. When you consider all the facts, I am solely to blame for her being gone. It kills me to think of it, but I have no choice. I have to find Ronald."

She has no idea just what lurks far below into the unknown. If only she could see what I see, Astrid thought, sinking into darker territory now. His thoughts plagued him like a curse. All he could see was Isra and how far she was away from him and how he couldn't get to her. Astrid knew better than to let his dark side get to him like this. He was stronger than he proclaimed to be. He had fought demons. Clashed against his foes in cloudy, darkened skies. Bold to be flying when perilous lighting flashed at him from every direction, a huge risk that he might have been struck by the fiery entity.

Silas nodded his head, feeling like he had heard all he needed and then arched his wings, unfurling them. He gazed at the sky for a moment before softly uttering, "Oh dear brother, I am not surprised at all this, but I don't feel there is much I can do. I've been with you all your life. I've helped you through many tribulations, alas now I cannot help any longer."

Astrid's face dropped in response. "If that is what you choose, I will have to respect it, but I don't understand why you'd desert me just when I need you the most," Astrid said. A puzzled expression fell over his face. Trying to understand Silas's reasoning was hard at the best of times, but he couldn't for the life of him comprehend why Silas would turn away now. "I guess I'll have to find the mortal myself. Let's face it, he's going to lead me straight to Isra," Astrid said.

"I am sorry," Silas bowed his head, backing away as he got into flight position.

Astrid watched quizzically with bewilderment. Silas left the scene, sweeping into the skies, hidden by the clouds as the night's cobalt blue covered him completely.

"Well, fine if he won't help, I'll deal with Ronald myself," Astrid remarked.

The air blurred around him as he was surrounded in black. Fiery sparks swirled around his masculine body, whirring as they spun around Astrid fantastically before finally grinding to a halt as they stopped, leaving him in his raven form.

I'll get even somehow, Astrid said sullenly to himself in thought. *I just don't know how yet. Ronald wants to take my witch from me. That's a step too far even for him. Oh, now it's time to really up the ante. He is going to know who I really am. He's going to discover the carnivorous monster in me.*

19

Dawn had arrived. A warm glow emitted from the sky. The golden rays gently glided across the land to launch in the day. A raven drifted in and out of the white fluffy clouds, bright eyed and buzzing with energy. His black wings were dazzling and shiny as they glided in the morning light.

The raven swooped down, hovering above the luscious landscape before him, a blur of yellow and green pasture. Sunny crocuses poked their tiny heads out amongst the grassy meadow decorated by sweet violets. The quaint little garden was tucked away in the outskirts of a wilderness

The raven scanned the area carefully, keeping his eyes peeled for a gray castle. That was his reason for coming here, although he couldn't see anything resembling a castle near him. Hmmm, he'd have to keep searching, for it must be somewhere around.

He slowed himself down to get a clearer view. His citrine eyes glowed as he flew lower, getting closer to the amber colored terrain. One eye fixed on the lime meadow abreast with flora while the other looked around and ahead of him. Behind this exquisite garden were acres of highland hills covered in the finest fern-green grass. As he veered closer toward the hills, he caught sight of a tall building, one a horrid, dull gray color.

The raven smiled. This had to be the place. He had said it was barely accessible and hidden away from the world. He flew over, swiftly landing on the soft grass, making a quiet landing. He maneuvered himself to the door, grasping the handle with his beak and willing it to fly open. He entered the castle, observing that the decadent walls in pomegranate finished with gilded gold framing were just like they were the last time he was here. He gracefully climbed the golden staircase to the top floor.

The raven used his beak to push past a royal blue curtain, giving him entry in the room that was hidden behind it. A red cushioned chair rested against the midnight-blue wall. Upon the chair reading an old, tattered book was a man. He had black hair, short but slicked back at the front but long enough to cover the base of his forehead. Moon-shaped glasses hung off his nose as he peeked at the raven with intrigued fascination.

"So, you're back, Astrid?" the man inquired. A wistful look of curiosity lay in his eye. He closed the book with his right hand, placing it on the window ledge beside him.

"Yes," Astrid cawed. He swerved over to the red chair, sitting beside the man. A sense of admiration could be noticed as he joyfully stood on his claws.

"And what did you learn?" the man asked, placing a finger on his lip, awaiting some tasty diligent detail that he wasn't sure he wanted to hear. But still he pressed on with his line of questioning. It was important to him.

The man, Samuel, worried about Astrid, the young raven, for he was a reckless soul. Rebelling against what society deemed he must do and choosing his own path was what he'd chosen to do. That path was quite often the dark one, a way of living that was frowned upon for a raven to be undertaking. Astrid was no exception to this as he often found himself placated into things he could not get out of. He'd gotten himself way too deep of a dark hole more than once and someone would have to retrieve him back into the lighter way of being.

Astrid, despite his misdemeanors, had been taught wisely by those closest to him the secrets of living a happy life. Samuel was Astrid's master and friend and had been accommodating Astrid's every need and whim since he had found the raven lurking about his castle with the news that he had no habitual home or friends he could rely on. He was a loner raven which Samuel found riveting as he had presumed ravens swarmed together in groups. How wrong he was.

Samuel was concerned for Astrid because he had been acting distant in recent times. Not his usual self as he would go gallivanting out into the night without a second word to Samuel, neither did he ask permission before leaving.

Astrid cleared his throat before blurting, "The young witch has come of age. She is nineteen years old now."

Samuel smiled, for he knew what was coming next. Forbidden fruit came to mind, something so deadly that it would be perilous to anyone that went near it. In this case, it was her, a female.

"Yes, she has," Samuel agreed. He wasn't going to argue over the facts. He paused before submitting, "But she's rooted in dark forces. She's covered in them by her own inception. They rush over her like warm blood flowing over a corpse." Samuel already knew that this wasn't going to go down well.

"I disagree," Astrid concurred. "There could still be a chance. I'd like to help her..." he said, quietly trailing off. "If she'll accept my help," he murmured quietly to himself.

Samuel glared at Astrid although his look was warm and caring. "Do you think someone as ghastly as Lady Isra of the Dark is wanting assistance? Especially coming from a light bearer such as yourself?"

Astrid shrugged that off. Even someone truly dark and embodied in evil can still want help at some point in her life. "She hasn't inherited that title, 'Lady' Isra of the Dark yet," Astrid asserted, looking toward Samuel.

Samuel's sky-blue eyes were affixed onto Astrid's in a stern frown.

"But she will. The prophecy said she'd turn her own heart inside out, ripping it from her own chest and inviting in the darkness. You saw it yourself. Don't deny that you saw it because you know it is true. Of course, I understand that you'd rather things turned out differently."

While he was going to be sullen with Astrid, he certainly didn't want to harm the young raven's feelings. He'd had an interest in the young sorceress since he had laid eyes on her. Samuel knew this wasn't just some idle crush and Astrid wasn't some hapless teenager. Astrid clearly had set his sights on her. Samuel couldn't help but feel Astrid was backing a losing horse so to speak, as light beings and dark forces rarely calibrated as one.

Astrid piped up eagerly. "I don't feel she is ghastly as you phrase it. I feel she is one that has gone into the lands of the dark with the ideal that she can shy away from all good. I believe there is potential in her. I won't lose hope."

Samuel said nothing, only smiled.

~ Present Day~

Astrid brushed away a tear as the memory faded. He had defended Isra that day, believing that she wouldn't always be drawn to the dark. He remembered stating to Samuel that he wasn't going to give up on her, no matter what happened.

He had only met her once when she was seventeen, brokenhearted, tears staining her porcelain skin as she cried over a man who didn't care for her. But yet the betrayal cut deep into her veins. The pain of it was so blinding that she had shunned away from her peers in favor of a quiet hideaway beside her favorite oak tree. Weeping over this man that had callously tore her heart from her, left her grief stricken.

Astrid had quietly shifted beside her and watched as she wept. She recalled over and over again how the man had taken her for granted, wanting her at first to be someone he wanted to be more acquainted with before deciding that he didn't want her at all. She was confused, rejected, lost in the midst of adolescence, struggling to contain the vile feelings that surged through her.

She finally stopped weeping after noticing Astrid. He said nothing to her, for he didn't want her to be startled by his voice, although he knew she was exceptionally in tune with the magic of the world they both dwelled in and wouldn't have been frightened by his ability to speak. Astrid still felt silence was best. He sat as she patted his head tenderly, feeling comforted merely by his presence.

She said something out loud that he would always remember: "Why am I always the one that falls for those that simply do not want to love me?"

He wanted to respond to her, but he knew he couldn't. He wanted to reassure her by uttering in his kindest tone of voice, "But don't you see? You are loveable. You just have to believe it."

Sure, Isra was far from reachable at the time, but still things beyond all hope could still be saved. He was hoping that he would be able to save her now. That would be a small comfort that would heal some pain inside his heart. He hoped that wherever Isra was, he would be able to get to her in time.

ASTRID BRISKLY STRODE THROUGH the clearing near to where Ronald O'Kutte resided. The bold trees were covered in frost. Astrid wore a black cloak, covering his head so that Ronald wouldn't know who he was. The home of Ronald O'Kutte lurked in a clearing hidden behind a group of overgrown pine trees, a quaint little cottage on its own island covered in soft white snow.

How ironic he chooses to hide himself here. It's not very sporting for a warrior-wannabe-warlock who yearns for such a life of prestige and power, Astrid remarked to himself.

Astrid laughed, feeling somewhat bemused, his black boots sinking into the snow. He hadn't even noticed winter was here. The icy, cold white carpet looked fresh and new so Astrid presumed it must have arrived very recently, for it seemed like autumn was only here yesterday.

Oh, how so much has happened since she has been gone! he thought quietly.

Astrid moved closer to the cottage, walking up what was the dull, gray path before the snow had arrived. He spotted some purple roses gracing an elegant door frame.

"How cute!" he marveled. A sharp sarcastic tone was in his voice, although now was not the time for criticism of Ronald's taste in floral decoration.

Astrid edged over to the door, noticing the violet-colored roses were growing horizontally around the window frames. Their rich purple color was now murky and the petals drooping. Lifeless and lacking moisture, they disintegrated in Astrid's fingers.

"Overgrown and left to wilt. I wonder what the inside of his home is like. This is hardly an extravagant palace!" Astrid chuckled, fearing the irony would be lost on Ronald. For a warrior, he was unkempt and disorganized.

THUMP! He pounded on the door, feeling disappointed the fragile wood didn't even splinter. Astrid was pretty angry. The door was his punching bag until he laid his eyes, or perhaps more accurately his fists, on Ronald. Oh, how he couldn't wait to get up close to him to inspect this mortal who had so foolishly, without due care, set his greedy mitts upon Lady Isra. He'd pay for that if nothing else.

How strange, there was no answer. Ronald must be at home. *Come on don't hide from me, boy,* Astrid thought sullenly to himself.

He hurled his fist upon the door again. *THUMP! THUMP!* It was so loud that Astrid was sure he could hear the sounds of timid feet from the next room, right from where he stood at the front of the cottage, frantic pacing footsteps, sounding like someone was coming. The sound grew closer. The footsteps grew more prominent as someone could be heard shuffling over to the door.

"Perfect. And it's about time!" Astrid said, feeling triumphant.

Astrid stood impatiently awaiting the moment the door would

swing open and he would be greeted by that pale face with cold blue eyes and muddy blonde hair.

Ronald had the looks of a warrior, at least the face of righteousness he was for sure. But now with his recent entrapping of Lady Isra, he had made himself a hypocrite. This would be a sore blow if his father Charles O'Kutte was still living. Ronald had spent many years listening to Charles lecture his sons about what was right and how it was important to do the right thing in any predicament. Ronald had listened to these talks about doing "the right thing" by his father but now he had swung the other way. It makes one wonder what his dear old dad has to say about it.

Finally after what seemed like forever, a sharp click was heard. The lock unbolted from the other side, quickly opening. Ronald appeared a moment later, disheveled and in a state of undress. A blue shirt unbuttoned and open at the front showed his chest hair growing in the middle. His legs were bare and free from pants. An embarrassed look flushed across his cheeks when he looked down at his half-spared nudity. Ronald gawped open mouthed at Astrid, bemused he had visitors at this hour.

"It's late, stranger. Wait, do I know you?" he muttered, sounding as if he had just woken.

Astrid pulled his black hood down, revealing his shimmery black hair. Short and trimmed at the sides, it gave him perfect sideburns in contrast with his beard that was also black.

"In a manner of speaking," Astrid revealed cryptically to Ronald.

"Oh?" Ronald's head turned sideways, inquisitive as to whom this stranger might be.

"I'm someone who has a piquing interest in the netherworld..." Astrid announced, licking his lips hurriedly, trying to decipher if he was getting anywhere with this engaging chatter he was stimulating.

Astrid wasn't entirely confident Ronald was buying his act. He had to admit he was enjoying himself. The blood twirled like a vortex in his veins, palms twitching with nervous and excited anticipation. The mortal looking back at him was receptive and accepting of the situation.

"...and in witches," Astrid dropped in suddenly.

Ronald paused. The blue coldness in his eyes that he possessed seemed bolder all of a sudden. Curiosity befell him in intriguing wonderment as if he was hanging on every syllable of the word "witches." His mouth twitched wildly as if considering something at the forefront of his mind, but he said nothing.

Astrid noted Ronald was silently thinking and perusing every single word Astrid uttered to him very selectively before he opened his mouth in response. Astrid surveyed Ronald carefully as he stood in front of him. Those bold brown eyes traveled down Ronald's form quizzically, studying him.

Ronald looked up, not giving Astrid eye contact and refusing to acknowledge him. He glared at the floor, as if looking for a salvation that might be found on his gravel pathway. Feeling intimidated and out of his depth, it was more than he cared to be truthful about.

"Witches are like a deadly ailment. It kills you slowly. I'm afraid I don't have much interest in them," Ronald mumbled. The lie emitted fire inside his body. He knew he was lying to this strange man, but something inside him did not want to admit the truth. He didn't want somebody he didn't know being inside his truths.

Ronald was trembling as he spoke. The heat poured from his body, leaving him dizzy. He imagined sweat dripping down his knees. It was pooling around the soles of his feet. Of course, it wasn't. Only in his illusion it was. His mind was carrying him away to another plane of existence as he stood trying to fathom his own polluted thoughts.

Ronald wanted to turn away, feeling the burn of Astrid's intrusion. It wasn't like he could escape this frightening man who had shown up at his doorstep out of the blue. He wasn't sure what to say, but it didn't matter, for Astrid was reading every molecule inside of him. He felt it as he finally looked up at Astrid's face, those penetrative eyes scorching through him.

"Yes, for sure," Astrid interrupted. "But I'm interested in one witch in particular." He stopped mid-conversation awaiting some sign from Ronald that he had his attention.

It was hard to distinguish if he had Ronald caught in the loop yet. but he wasn't going to give up easily. Astrid was determined to hook the boy by the balls even if it meant giving into his own reckless power. Astrid mulled through his mind chatter as he stood watching Ronald. Lady Isra was the reason for him coming here in the wilderness like this to seek out Ronald. She was his reason for sliding down into a blackened Hell, if he was going there.

But saying that, Astrid was cautious. It wasn't something he wanted to disclose immediately. Astrid had to execute this while being slick in his manner, as though he had a lucky hand of cards. Careful and strategic while looking over at his opponent, he studied his facial expressions and body language, analyzing them to see if Ronald would break before he did.

Then again, Astrid was used to this way of life. Being cautious and creeping around, not revealing his intentions in things until he knew for sure he was undertaking the right course of action. Diving down into every single detail, Astrid always checked everything over, making sure everything was as it appeared to be. That was simply how he worked.

Ronald said nothing. Still not a single word came out of his mouth. His lips were dry and beginning to crack from the strain of the pressure he was under. Surely, he'd have to break the silence soon or perhaps Astrid would be standing here all night. If only Ronald could say something and put himself out of this dull aching silence. It was wishful thinking, but Ronald was as quiet as a gray gargoyle statue. His breathing stalled; it could barely be heard, like he was holding his breath.

Astrid was still keeping his beady eye on Ronald, searching for any sign of life in the man, although that was more like a pun because he was standing so perfectly straight. Some would think him elegant as he stood so poignantly. But no, he wasn't moving an inch nor making a sound. Astrid was beginning to think that Ronald had been trained to be that way, to address one's enemies with nothing but deadly silence to keep the pressure off his own person. And he figured that kind of tactic would probably work too, if it wasn't Astrid facing off with him.

Ha, who would have thought it, Ronald O'Kutte lost for words. Now this really is a novelty. Bet the villagers would screech with laughter if they could see him now. Some warrior he is. He can't even face me! This man can't even bring himself to tear me down while I eyeball him at his doorstep. Are you a man or a mouse, my friend?

Astrid resisted the urge to chuckle to himself although he really wanted to. *The boy isn't far from cracking,* Astrid thought to himself, highly amused at the fact that his little game was getting to the mortal. But he always found hilarity in small things. "Well?" Astrid motioned to Ronald.

"Well? What?" Ronald questioned, seeming annoyed that Astrid was still interrogating him on his front porch.

"Aren't you interested to know who she is?" Astrid pressed.

"Er, no. Sorry. I find witches to be what my father would describe as an unwilling invitation down to the pits of death. And when you get to the bottom they'll swallow you whole in one gulp. That's how vindictive and clever they are!" Ronald expressed, finally breaking the dull silence.

"It sounds like you know far more than you claim to," Astrid remarked. Spit emitted from his mouth in anger. Oh, he was so close to getting this mortal entwined in his deadly web. It was only a matter of time before he got the chance to drag him away, somewhere nice and quiet where not a soul could hear him.

Come on boy, just admit it, Astrid thought to himself.

He was getting impatient now. His fingers twitched on both hands. His skin was just itching to get a taste of dark paradise, that delightful feeling he got in his veins when he launched his vengeance and got what he came for. The rush of the excitement felt so amazingly good, he couldn't even begin to describe it. The sensation he had when he was about to strike down and catapult his victim into cruel torture beyond anything they had ever felt in all their lifetimes elated him.

"I know many things, stranger," Ronald clarified. He stopped as he turned to think about what was coming next. "I know a witch destroyed my family. My brother Kane disappeared after he sought a particular witch out. I think her name was Inna or Isma or something like that."

Astrid glared at Ronald. Oh, that was it. That was it! Trying to pretend he couldn't remember Isra's name, oh golly, he was really going to be in for it now. Astrid forced his hands into fists, squeezing the life out of his flesh, trying to contain his rage.

Prepare to have all manner of Hell unleashed onto you! I just cannot wait to take you away from here. I just can't wait to watch you rot for everything you've done to her. I am compelled to put you through so much pain that you'll be begging for forgiveness just to stop yourself screaming, Astrid mulled over silently to himself. His thoughts once again had gone to realms of terror that he could only relish while Ronald would get to relive them over and over again.

"But my brother was never seen again. Many say she killed him," Ronald continued.

Astrid had to keep his cool although he wanted to rip the life out of Ronald piece by piece starting with that irritating mouth of his. Oh yes, he'd get rid of that first, if only to stop that vexatious drivel that came trickling from his lips. He'd shred every limb from that wreck of a human carcass until poor Ronald was on his knees, hanging onto his very last breath.

"I see," Astrid said. He was trying to be calm and collected.

But how to move this little debacle on to a phase in which he and Ronald were in more familiar territory?

I need to hook him, Astrid thought, *but how? How do I get him so agreeable that he comes along with me, doing exactly how I wish?*

"Yes. But it's no issue of mine. Witches always get what is meant for them in the end," Ronald voiced.

Astrid glared across at him. How dare he! He was implying that Isra deserved whatever was happening to her. Sure, she had gone and kept the boy Kane for a while, but she didn't kill him.

Don't get it wrong, her way of dealing with Kane was extreme on many levels but she didn't kill him. I know because I was there, Astrid thought angrily. *You fucking did, Ronald! You murdered your own brother in cold blood. Now what sort of a man does that make you, eh?*

Oh, how Astrid wanted to scream that from the bellows. How would he react knowing he killed his own brother hidden away in a furry suit? He was betting it wouldn't go down too well. The color would probably drain from the so-called warrior's pale face.

"I'm guessing you know all that. Witches getting what they deserve, that is," Astrid said calmly. He was doing his utmost not to overreact.

"Let's just say, she's in for something she will never ever forget," Ronald said coolly.

"Interesting. So, you took care of her? This witch?" Astrid pressed.

"Yes. I have to find some retribution for my family. I can't claim back my brother's life, but her life hanging in the balance will have to suffice," Ronald retorted. His lips pressed together in a smirk. He was enjoying this. The little fiend was entertained and it was written all over his face.

"Hmm," Astrid said in response. It was harder than he thought having to be nice to this parasite, especially when he wanted to take him here and now.

Astrid took a deep breath, a fake half smile suddenly gracing his face. He even seemed somewhat calm. How he managed that in the heat of the moment, not even he could explain. He was raging inside. The violence swirled inside his stomach like a vortex, whirring round and round. It was almost as if Astrid was going to be sick. The feeling surged all through his intestinal tract, overwhelming him as he fought to stop everything, he had barely eaten from the last couple of hours from making reappearance.

"That's totally understandable in regard to the circumstances you mentioned," Astrid replied.

Astrid twitched his eyebrow quizzically. The anger was blowing up inside him. All he wanted to do was to grab Ronald and smack the life out of him, but he couldn't. He had to be calm and cool about it . If he flipped now, all chances to find Isra would be lost. He wanted Ronald's hands to be tied so that he'd say anything to get out of it.

Astrid wanted Ronald to feel trapped so that he'd say or do anything to save his own rotten skin.

It was time for Astrid to make his move. He had been standing there long enough going along with his polite charade. It had been twenty minutes ago Astrid had sought Ronald out on his doorstep although it seemed like hours. Astrid was getting antsy. One of them had to swing this around and move it along. He presumed he was the one that would have to do it. And do it he would, with sincere pleasure.

"Say...." Astrid plastered on a fake smile, making out he was cheery and all about the joys of spring. Pausing mid-conversation, he waited to see if Ronald was going along with it or not, and then said, "I have a proposition for you. I think maybe you can claim your brother back after all. But we can't discuss it here. Let's go somewhere quiet where we can have a nice long chat," Astrid suggested.

Wow, I can't believe I just said that. Is he dumb enough to fall for that? Maybe since I'm all dressed in black, he will assume I'm a warlock or something, Astrid pondered.

Ronald's mouth dropped in shock. His left hand clapped over his mouth in horror. Ronald stepped out of his home, careful to shut the door firmly behind him. If there was going to be something happening here, he sure as hell wasn't going to have it occur in his home.

No, this couldn't be true. Kane was gone. Surely there was no way of getting him back. Kane had been taken by a witch and there was no undoing that. But here a stranger was, telling him that just perhaps something could be done. And Ronald was willing to take the chance that resolution could finally be found. The needless matter of Lady Isra had slipped his mind. Ronald had almost forgotten what he'd done to her. The sudden whim of him finding Kane again was pressing enough to keep his mind busy.

Astrid grinned back at Ronald. The raven-man had obviously been reading Ronald's thoughts. *I've got you now, boy,* he chuckled mercilessly to himself, amused by how taken Ronald was by his super quick elaborated plan.

"Okay," Ronald said, staring Astrid in the eyes. "I'll go along with you." He added, "If, on the off chance that my brother is alive, will you do something for me?" Ronald felt optimistic and hopeful. This stranger had magically come to him, giving him what he needed, thus restoring his faith in humankind.

"Of course," Astrid replied, rubbing his hands eagerly in anticipation for what was coming.

"Will you make Lady Isra finally face what she has done?" Ronald pressed. He wasn't smiling. The redness on his face resembled the wicked anger vibrating through his soul.

"You can count on it," Astrid lied through gritted teeth.

Ronald O'Kutte was about to regret the very day he had been brought to this earth. Off he walked with this person he believed to be a stranger down a path that would lead him to the greatest mortal peril he would ever live to experience. That's *if* he managed to live to tell his ghastly tale.

20

~ Three Years Ago~

A sharp chime sounded. The stroke of midnight came much closer than had been anticipated. A raven waited in the shadow of night. His silhouette stood out in between the mossy green grass, softly blending into the cobalt-blue sky like a watercolor.

The raven seemed nervous while he sat perched on a grey and white cobblestone wall. Gruesome sap-colored mold grew in between the cracks, glowing in the darkness like fireflies. The bright green color shone for everyone to see.

The raven arched its back, preparing to sweep into the air. He ruffled his feathers anxiously, tense as he knew it was almost time to leave here. He didn't want to go, but he knew if he didn't, things could happen that he didn't want. Serious implications would occur as a result of him interfering with fate and he sure as hell was not going to mix it up with that.

Although this journey was unwanted, he knew he had to meet his maker. No, he wasn't going to be facing life's end. This was a different kind of maker, if you'll pardon the expression. The raven was hoping his actions would be excused, pondering his apologies for going against what he had been told to do.

"She may be worth this rebellion. I have to take the chance," he said to himself, in flight.

Towering above the landscape that appeared to be so tiny in his bird's eye view, he searched for his destination, a tall gray castle where he was due to meet the man in question, Samuel, the man who took care of him and in some ways owned him, although he never claimed it.

Why be owned if they won't control you? Samuel doesn't lock me in a cage, however I am held to the righteous rules of this world in which the magical and mystical come together in a beautiful merging of fantastical light, the raven thought to himself.

Seeing his destination clearly in front of him, he headed downward. He set his eyes forward in preparation to land, fixed on the gray building. The brick building had metal spires in gilded gold almost reaching the top of the sky. Black iron frames decorated every window. Pale, drawn out curtains could be seen from the outside. A lightness shown within this place of magic and mystery.

Astrid the raven had been here many times in his lifetime, although this was his first time visiting in several years. Feeling like he was coming back to a wreck, he sighed. He was a ghost in his own home about to unleash the past under his feet. So much time had passed since Astrid had laid eyes on Samuel. He'd left in a vile huff because Astrid felt that Samuel didn't understand his reasoning. Having been told that Astrid couldn't do this because it was against the universal law, the same one he had been born into several years ago upset him.

Astrid seemed nervous as he landed on the window ledge. Slipping in through the glass quietly, he turned his head around upon entering, checking that no one had spotted him. Taking sight of the stone staircase, he began climbing it. His claws hit each step as he went up, and finally he reached the top level.

Taking a deep breath at the final step, he inched forward. There was no more time to prepare. This was it. There was nothing left to do except face it. Pushing through the royal blue curtain, Astrid crept in, feeling foreshadowed as he stood in the middle of the room, almost awaiting his doom.

Out of nowhere, it came. A hardened voice so loud it echoed across the room. "Astrid!" it called out sternly.

Orange flames shimmered around a tall pillar candle. A solemn face could only just be made out in the pitch black. Cold eyes stared around in circles, penetrating the icy atmosphere in the room. Moon-framed glasses in silver were complimentary to his eyes. He sat awkwardly in his red cushioned chair. His back pressed against it as if he had been sitting here for quite a while, waiting for this moment.

Astrid looked up at Samuel. His head bent down to honor his master. "Samuel," he acknowledged. The air was still and quiet as he spoke. The coldness of the room seemed even stronger now.

Astrid stood, nervously awaiting a reply. It was one thing to come here like this after eleven years of avoiding this place. Astrid didn't know if he would be welcomed with open arms or whether he'd be killed. He had gone against all that was divine, after all. His purpose. The spiritual mission he had been born into. He had abandoned it to seek out a witch. Now that really was rebelling in its finest form if ever one had existed.

"You've been away for a long time!" Samuel coaxed gently.

Astrid bent his head, feeling guilty of his absence. "Yes, I have, but if you please..."

"SILENCE!" Samuel bellowed. He wasn't amused.

Here was Astrid, a fine fellow led to do well and be good, and yet he was turning his back on it. Samuel could barely contain his anger. How could Astrid lose himself in a quest for a witch of all horrid creatures? Every lightbeing knew that witches were wicked through and through. Only poison ran through their veins, deadly serum that leaked through their hearts, cursing everything it was spilled onto. But Astrid had paid that no mind.

"I know what you are going to say," Samuel countered. "Chasing after that witch? I'm not stupid, Astrid. I foresaw this years ago when you laid eyes on her the first time around."

Astrid's heart sank a little. He wasn't sure how he was going to articulate this to Samuel. It was one of those situations where it was best to simply say how you feel, but doing it could land you into trouble, almost like a double-edged sword. Someone was bound to get hurt, but Astrid wasn't going to be swayed.

"She's killed the dragon, turning to the darkness like the prophecy said she would," Astrid blurted before looking down at the floor once more, feeling his master would be less than pleased about his admission.

Samuel looked at Astrid, almost burning him with his stare. His bold eyes scorched every molecule of Astrid's being, closely examining every inch of his body, mind, and soul.

"Yes, well I can't pretend to be shocked there, boy. You were told of this coming long ago," Samuel said, blunt as always. His words sounded like ash, as if he was cursing every syllable as it expelled from his lips. "And I suppose I know what's coming next, don't I?"

Samuel motioned and pressed a finger cautiously to his lips, holding a pause. The entire room fell silent. Astrid stood motionless, not sure whether he should proceed. The silence between him and Samuel made him tremble a little. Still, he wasn't going to let this stand in his way. Even if it meant him and Samuel would part ways, Astrid was determined to do what he had set out, and that was finding his happiness. Above all else, what more could one want in life? Being happy and content with the things in his life was the ultimate goal. So sacrifices would be made and he'd live with the consequences of his decisions as he had always done.

"I'm going to her. Tonight," Astrid voiced, checking Samuel's face for signs. He wanted to ensure he didn't offend Samuel if at all possible.

"I figured as much, boy," Samuel countered.

He looked like he was going to say something else but stopped. Samuel lowered the finger from his lips. He turned to the window as if looking for some inspiration to say the right thing and not be angry with his charge, because no matter what Astrid did, Samuel didn't want to hurt his feelings.

"You always were one to rebel against what nature deemed right in the eyes of the light. So tell me, what happens when she learns who you are? When she hears of your sordid part in this masquerade?" Samuel questioned.

Astrid maneuvered over to the dusty black window ledge and allowed his eyes to meet Samuel's in an emotional glance. A tear gently swept down Astrid's face, dropping onto the floor. He had a knowing this would be the last time he conversed with Samuel and something within him wasn't at all okay about that. He knew after this there was no going back.

"I know you don't understand my reasoning, Samuel, but I must do this. I still think she can be saved," he expressed softly.

Years of wanting and yearning for the witch's heart were finally coming undone at the seams. He had desires beyond what even she could muster, but she would not have any knowing that she was one of them until he felt that she could handle it and be open to loving him.

"I understand completely."

Samuel swallowed as he spoke. He knew he would have to speak the truth. If he didn't, he could never be at peace. Astrid would be told and then it would be at his discretion whether he decided to dive into this whirlpool of a witch's torn heart or not.

Presumably Astrid would go on his way to her, no matter what Samuel said to dissuade him. Samuel knew Astrid better than he knew himself. When this raven had set his mind to something, that would be it. There would be no changing it and it wouldn't matter how much bluster and chaos was placed in his way. He would still forfeit everything he held dear.

"But the painful thing is, Lady Isra is beyond reprieve. She doesn't know love or companionship. In fact, my dearest light heart, you'd be best not going to her at all. For I can only feel heartache emerging as a result of your deep seating longing for this ... dark creature. She won't love you, not the way you love her. Ever."

"Perhaps she may in time," Astrid started, his voice almost a whisper.

"She darkened her heart. Love cannot be found when one's heart is truly blackened," Samuel said quietly. Besides, she has no recollection of you or anything that commenced, so you'd be best forgetting about it."

Astrid said nothing. He glanced over to the landscape outside. Vast greenery stretched out for miles covered in sweet, shaded violet. The gray castle was the only thing amongst all the brightened colors that was shrouded in dark despite the light that was hidden inside. Beauty is a terrible thing when love is lacking. There is no wonder without love. When there is no love to be found in a place, nothing can grow.

Samuel straightened himself, smiling at his charge for a moment. Relentless foreboding pummeled through his body. His arms felt limp and heavy as a painful sensation ripped through his skin. The anxiety of being a man, held up to do duty was never easy, especially when that duty meant letting go of someone he truly cared for.

Finally, Samuel spoke. "There is a way, but it must not be taken lightly. In three years' time when the sun marries the moon in a cataclysm of light battling dark, a new dawn will arrive. Your witch will get her promised salvation, but I can't promise that it will be forever. She will face everything she has ever done in a violent fury surpassed by blackened torment that only she will see. I cannot guarantee her immortality, nor can I claim that she will awaken once it takes hold. However, you will know it has commenced when the black rose is discovered in your lands. Now go, Astrid. You must never return. I forbid you from coming back to this place. That is all. Go."

Astrid nodded before turning to the open window. Not giving Samuel a second glance, he sighed. Lifting himself up, he fluttered his wings. Not saying a word, he flew out into the cold-hearted skies.

~ Present Day~

Astrid smiled, remembering Samuel's words. Although Samuel had got most of his prophecy surrounding Isra wrong, some of it had been factually accurate. Despite her misgivings over the light and what she fondly referred to as the love and light brigade, Isra's heart had allowed love in.

He sighed, wondering what it would be like if Samuel was here now. Three years had passed since those famous last words Samuel had said to Astrid. Would he have reprimanded his former raven protégé, or maybe marvel at the man Astrid had become, proud of him for standing so firm in his human carcass? Or maybe Samuel would be brass in scolding Astrid for getting so entwined with the dark forces in his and Isra's world. Who would have known since Samuel wasn't there to give his opinion? It would have to stay unresolved.

Astrid reminisced, forgetting himself. Realizing he had company, he broke his reverie. He glanced back at his soon-to-be captive.

Ronald looked up at Astrid. The raven-man's mouth curled into a sly smile. It was intriguing for Ronald to meet someone who knew so little about him, but yet was prepared to give him what he wanted when there was nothing to be gained in return.

"I presume you know her? The witch, I mean?" Ronald gushed.

"In a manner of speaking," Astrid said with no emotion. He wasn't going to let on the real truth just yet. It would be more fun to lead Ronald astray first, to toy with his selfish yearning of revenge that he was never going to see.

"Ah, so where are we going?" Ronald inquired. He slowly trailed behind Astrid.

They had been walking for just over an hour now. Ronald was curious to see where this would eventually lead. Getting his hands on Lady Isra was one thing. Having someone lead him straight to her was like a gift wrapped in the finest silks that only he would have the pleasure of unwrapping.

"A cottage in the woods," Astrid answered. He wasn't giving anything away.

One word and short answers had been his forte ever since he had convinced Ronald to go off with him on this dangerous trek into the unknown. He was keeping quiet, only speaking when Ronald had asked a question and that had been for most of the duration of their walk.

If Ronald were as intelligent as he had claimed to be, he would have realized that Astrid was laughing at him all the way. A sly grin was plastered across his face as if he had struck gold all of a sudden. A coldness resided in his soul that made him joyful, almost skipping all the way to his little secret hideaway he was taking Ronald to. Astrid couldn't let out his violent passion that made him so wonderfully content, not yet. All he could do was smile secretly to himself because all good things had to be delicately served ice cold to be at their ultimate best.

"Ah, isn't it dangerous for you, trying to claim yourself a witch?" Ronald asked. His curiosity piqued once more.

"No," Astrid voiced. There was no feeling in his voice.

Astrid turned to Ronald, almost smiling. A wicked expression formed across his facial features. Fire burned in his brown eyes, keeping his smile intact. He licked his lips smugly as though he was about to sink his teeth into something delicious and revel in the taste. He wanted to savor the moment for what it was.

"Everyone has their darkness, boy. Lady Isra of the Dark is mine," Astrid said wickedly.

Licking his lips once again before turning away from Ronald, that evil sinister smile grew bigger as Ronald once again fell into Astrid's treacherous hook, lapping up every word the bold raven-man had to say.

21

Astrid smiled, feeling pleased with himself. Stood in the darkened room where not a soul could hear anything, he turned to his terrified houseguest. Ronald O'Kutte sat on the floor, petrified at what was going to happen next. Ropes bound his hands together as he sat awkwardly in a cross-legged position awaiting his fate.

Astrid had led him here, to this abandoned cottage out in the woods on the false pretense that he was going to lure Lady Isra here. A clever lie, of course, because Astrid's intentions were far greater than that.

Ronald had merrily gone along with the idea until Astrid had gotten him through the doorway, sealing it shut with a powerful enchantment that not even Ronald could have broken. For a man so obsessed with being a warlock, he wasn't too bright.

"So you tricked me, knowing who I was? Luring me here with the idea that you'd destroy the woman who wreaked havoc unto my family?" Ronald spat angrily.

"Yes, yes, I did. But you weren't aware of who I am. You still aren't," Astrid mocked.

He stopped, sliding himself across the back of a wooden chair. His

165

arms clasped the back firmly and he sat upright while he turned to face his prisoner. "You thought I was going to let you have your wicked way with her? Oh boy, you're more stupid than I had assumed. But it is your lust for greed and power that landed you in my web. Silly fool!"

Ronald looked on speechless, feeling quite stupid that he had fallen for Astrid's conniving plan. If only he had wizened up when Astrid began telling him why he was seeking Isra out! But no, the silly boy was so dead set on revenge on the woman who had made it so that he had to grow up that he'd lost sight of reality. A magickal man at heart, he was still unable to see through a half truth.

If his father could see him now ... what a waste of a life.

Astrid smiled, licking his lips triumphantly. "You know, I've had a real rough few days. I think you and I should chat." He motioned angrily, still smiling because he was the one in control.

Ronald grunted. "It could be worse, I suppose. What are you going to do to me?" he questioned, feeling the burn of the rope on the back of his hands.

Astrid stood up, looking down on Ronald, taunting him with his silence, barely saying a thing and not giving him the release he so desperately craved. It would be more fun to do this, to play with the poor boy a little before delivering him the most perfect gift that not even he could have concocted with his so-called magicks!

"First of all, we must talk from one man to another," Astrid started.

"Oh, how delightful, a nice little chat," Ronald emitted with desperation.

The smile had not faded from Astrid's face. He was going to enjoy every second of this. This power of being able to dominate others' emotions was far greater than any curse. Manipulating a person using their desires merged with their weaknesses, it didn't get any better than that.

Some humans are so stupid. They see what they want to see, plunging ahead full force with a yearning for greatness and sustaining themselves in a false identity of being in control when really someone else is pulling their strings from behind the mirror. Oh, how incredibly silly!

Astrid's thoughts of torture stopped. His mind fast-tracked to Isra. *Where is she? I have to know where she is. I must find her, even if it means wrenching myself into chaotic darkness by what I may have to do. But I'll do whatever it takes to get back to her, but first I must unleash this mortal's deadly truth unto him.*

"I believe you had a brother," Astrid countered.

Ronald's face dropped in shock that Astrid would go as far to mention his brother, the one Lady Isra had murdered in cold blood ... or that was what he had chosen to believe.

"Yes, the wicked witch of Shambre Fell destroyed his life. She killed his nearest and dearest, sweet Lillian, before killing him after she handed him the truth," Ronald concurred.

Astrid folded his arms. A stern look formed across his face and the smile vanished like a dream that had been catapulted into a nightmare. "And how would you be able to stumble across the news of Lillian?" Astrid challenged.

Ronald squirmed. He grimaced as the rope rubbed horribly against his smooth skin. It was rough. He felt a burning sensation on his wrists. Ronald shuffled across the floor in the hope that changing his position would minimize the pain, but it was to no avail as he was still very uncomfortable.

Astrid watched closely, expecting an answer. "Well?!"

Ronald attempted to relocate himself on the floor by trying to turn himself around in the hope he would be less restricted in his movement, but with no luck. Astrid found it fascinating how a human that was severely impacted from going anywhere would still try and do so. The hope and determination Ronald had was astounding despite his predicament.

"A friend of Lady Isra's told me about Lillian. Or maybe she was a foe," Ronald remarked bluntly.

It all clicked into place in Astrid's head. There could only be one who had the power to know something like that when she was nowhere to be found in Isra's line of view. The fatefully vengeful one. The one that hated Isra as much as Isra had hated her. Everilda!

"Ah, our dearest Everilda making waves beyond the grave!" Astrid chuckled.

"Yes, well, the witch told me of how Lady Isra took Kane after refusing to give him what he sought her out for before taking it a step too far by going after Lillian," Ronald expressed. His face was sullen and full of regret.

Astrid straightened his stance, turning away from Ronald to look out upon the gardens through the clear glass. The red roses still grew favorably despite years of not being attended to. He found it ironic that things of beauty could still thrive here in Lillian's cottage after all these years.

"Yes, I know she killed Lillian. Although I felt it was extreme at the time, it was her choice," Astrid commented.

His face flushed as he remembered Isra stood over Lillian covered in that pungent red liquid. He was glad he hadn't witnessed the brutal killing itself. He certainly didn't need those kinds of nightmares.

Ronald shifted once more in his position, almost squirming, trying to gain some kind of imaginary comfort that wasn't there. He wasn't there to hear of Lillian's murder as he had been away at the time. He had only heard of it afterward since the villagers were talking about it incessantly. This was shortly after Ronald and his father Charles had realized Kane had disappeared. It had taken them a few months to notice, for Kane was always going off chasing one thing or another, never behaving the way he was supposed to. He didn't exactly act how a warrior born into a family of seers should be.

"And you think Lillian deserved to be killed?" Ronald questioned.

Astrid turned back to Ronald in a thoughtful glance. His arms dropped to his sides, still and quiet. "No. I don't..." He trailed off, realizing that it was a very dark time back then for Isra.

She had sought freedom in the world of death and destruction. That was her way of coping with the heartbreak she'd had years prior to this. After all, Astrid had been the one by her side when she had wept over a man who had crushed her heart in two. Not that Isra knew any of this. She probably assumed it was another raven, but it was Astrid.

"But I wasn't there. Only saw it once she had done it," Astrid added, a serious tone in his voice.

"All right, so you didn't agree with her doing it, is that what you are saying?" Ronald asked. He felt dumbfounded that someone so close to Isra wasn't okay with something she had done.

"Yes, that's what I am saying. As for your brother, I told her to let him go. I know for a fact that she did exactly that after she showed him Lillian."

Ronald looked bemused. How could this be? Lady Isra had killed Kane, he was sure of it. There was no other logical explanation. She had Kane's blood on her hands. He hadn't researched magicks and the occult for no reason. It was to get to her, to find this woman who had destroyed his family with one vile swoop.

"How do you know she let him go?" Ronald questioned. His face went pale as if he was about to hear something he didn't want to.

Astrid knelt down onto the floor beside Ronald. He stayed silent for a moment as he eyed the mortal man carefully. His gaze burned on the trembling man's form before he raised a hand to Ronald's chin, lifting it up, and replied, "Because your greedy brother came back three days after Isra showed him Lillian. I was there."

"Whoa! How did he manage that? How can that be?" Ronald was almost stuttering.

Astrid got up once again. Lifting himself from the floor, he smoothed the floor's dust from his trousers as if brushing away something disgusting.

"He came back, seeking out Isra again. I stopped him," Astrid muttered, remembering how Kane had been creeping in the gardens looking for Isra. "Luckily, I was the only one around or things might have gotten quite ugly; well, for Kane anyway."

Ronald's mouth dropped, shocked that his brother had indeed escaped the witch's clutches after all. Impossible it seemed, but the man so close to her would have no reason to lie, especially if he wanted her back safe and sound.

"How did you stop him?" Ronald asked. Afraid of the answer, he sat almost crying, his eyes getting ready to drip as if he was a fountain. The tears were bitter and salty as they piled up in his tear ducts awaiting a release.

"I told him there and then he shouldn't have come back. I didn't like his feeble excuse so I turned him into a black cat and presented him to Isra," Astrid confessed. The guilt on his face was clearly visible under a worried frown. His gaze was penetrating. The once confident and wicked smile went vacant from him.

Ronald started to cry. "But I thought that cat was hers!" he said through painful sobs. "Oh goodness, I can't believe it. I killed him, believing he was hers!!" Ronald exclaimed. If his hands weren't tied, he'd have punched the air with his fists. He was so angry with himself and Astrid for his involvement in it. *If only I had left things alone, Kane might still be alive,* he thought to himself.

"Isra is not to blame for that. She doesn't even know that Kane returned to Shambre Fell," Astrid explained. Feeling like a weight was lifted off his shoulders, he actually felt sorry for Ronald for a second.

This poor man believed he was handing out justice well served and had only gone and shot himself in the foot, wounding the already aching part of his loss even more so, for he had killed his brother. Not Isra. Not Astrid. It was him.

Suddenly a thought dawned on Ronald. He sat sullenly mulling it over inside his head. The information filtered through his brain as he began to put everything together from the night he'd arrived at Shambre Fell. He remembered it was a cold night, just after midnight. And there had been a sleeping cat in the grass.

Ronald edged closer to see it was black and furry. It quickly stirred awake. All of its fur stood on end as it stared at Ronald, shocked. Thinking about it, that cat was doing its utmost to get Ronald's attention. He'd found it annoying at the time, but now it began to make sense.

That cat was all over me like a rash! Oh my, what if he was trying to warn me? Trying to tell me all of this. What the hell have I done?

It didn't bear thinking about, but damn, it was all he could think about. If only he had stopped and listened instead of brutally murdering the poor creature. He had no desire to relive that moment, although Ronald did remember the way the cat looked as it laid there on the stone path, silent as if it was sleeping. The body was cold and the hair matted due to all the blood from where the animal had been mutilated. God, it was awful.

Ronald's head finally rose from his deep-thinking position, meeting Astrid's eyes in a cold, forlorn look. "So, all that time I thought she had enacted this terrible revenge, when my brother was actually under my nose I was the one that ended his life?!" he exclaimed.

"Well, now that the pleasantries are out of the way, we need to get to the matter at hand," Astrid muttered.

Astrid folded his arms and stood over Ronald stern and serious. He showed no emotion, shadowing Ronald like a wolf about to sink his teeth into his frightened prey. Astrid looked menacing from where he stood. His gaze burned into Ronald's eyes, waiting for the pitiful mortal to crack under the pressure. It was only a matter of time before he did.

Ronald said nothing which was unsurprising when you think of how much power Astrid had over the situation. You'd think Ronald would be squealing the knowledge away just to save his weasley skin, but no. He kept quiet.

It's no matter that you say nothing, Astrid thought. We'll do this the old-fashioned way. You wanted a witch, my boy, you got a witch but you got more than you bargained for this time. Now one way or another, I'm going to find her and you're going to tell me where she is!

"Isra!" Astrid barked. His voice sounded so loud it could have almost made the dainty glass window crack. Fiery and dangerous it was! "Where the hell is she?" Astrid questioned.

Astrid shot a dagger look in Ronald's direction. Ronald smirked for the first time since he'd been held captive by Astrid.

"Reliving all the hellish things she's ever done and it's all due to a simple black rose," he gloated.

Astrid looked at Ronald like he wanted to kill him. He envisioned himself wrapping his strong hands around Ronald's neck for a moment, holding just enough tension to make it painful, but not to crack it. Ronald wouldn't die like that, no. But he'd feel the pain like he'd never felt it and he'd be begging for Astrid to snap his precious human neck. That's for sure.

The thought whirled around inside Astrid for a moment until suddenly he noticed a tall man with slicked-back black hair stood in front of him. No, it couldn't be. Samuel? After all these years?

"Hello Astrid," Samuel started.

Astrid couldn't believe it. No, not Samuel, not the man who knew everything there was to know about Lady Isra and he knew Astrid pretty well, too.

"Samuel," Astrid gasped. He placed a hand to his mouth, masking the shock.

"I thought I'd make an appearance since things aren't going too well." Samuel motioned, looking down at Ronald. Samuel's bold blue eyes glinted across at Ronald as if he was something that shouldn't be in the scenario.

"Oh that. It's just some fodder," Astrid remarked. The sarcasm was fluent in his voice.

"Yes, well that fodder as you name him is causing all manner of reactions from on high," Samuel countered. Samuel folded his arms, trying to seem casual. He flashed a stern look in Astrid's direction.

"He's taken Isra," Astrid snarled. Gruffness was deep in his voice.

"Yes, I know. And I know where she is, but we won't get anywhere close to that until you find reasoning over this ... *human,*" Samuel muttered.

Astrid's mouth dropped open. He was almost speechless. He marched up to Samuel, leaving Ronald watching in disbelief. Ronald had no inclination as to what was happening between the two men, all he could fathom was that they knew each other well. It must be some connection for the older, sterner man to come all this way just to give Astrid a telling off.

"You know where she is? Tell me!" Astrid commanded.

He was so close in proximity to Samuel he could smell the man's whiskey breath, presumably from an early stress-relieving breakfast. Samuel had always been fond of the warm malt drink. He'd take a big gulp, letting the spicy liquid flow down to his insides. He found it a comforting feeling as if a fire had been lit inside the pit of his stomach.

Samuel saw how close Astrid was but didn't back away. He knew the raven-man was uncontrollable and that he could literally get in his face at any given moment. Samuel guessed it would not take much to make Astrid lose his temper, for he knew the man well, long before he was a man. Any excuse would suffice in order to satisfy Astrid's need for enacting his anger. Samuel knew that, so even though they had such a strong foundation under them, he would have to tread carefully to not upset Astrid.

"Yes, I know where she is," Samuel coaxed. "But we need to resolve things here before we can get to that."

He was speaking in his prim and professional manner in an attempt to calm Astrid. Having a rational approach was Samuel's ideal and he had known from previous experience that it had gone down like a storm with Astrid in getting him from being a surging fireball about to implode to someone that could be civilized and courteous.

"What do we have to resolve?" Astrid piped up.

It was piquing his inquiring mind in such a way that he could feel the cogs in his brain whirring with anticipation of what might be in store.

How intriguing. Samuel wants him and I to reconcile after three years of not uttering a single syllable to each other. There must be some reason he had come here to seek me out in this way. I wonder what it is, he thought silently to himself.

A snide grin displayed across Astrid's face while he thought of the possibilities.

Come on out with it, old man, we don't have all day. Isra needs me, so tell me where she is and then we can both go ahead with what we set out to do. He sounded impatient in his mind chatter, absently pattering on to himself and for a second forgetting that Samuel was still in front of him.

"Where do I start, Astrid? There's you in a union with Lady Isra after disobeying me. Then there's her disappearing as a result of the black rose emerging, and finally, we have you going unhinged at the man you believe is responsible when really this was all part of the plan," Samuel elaborated.

"But he's implicated her under his spell!" Astrid exclaimed. He looked angry. The redness on his cheeks was brash and filled with fury, like an atomic bomb that had been sitting too long, waiting to explode.

"Yes, he did, but this was all part of the plan. It doesn't matter about whom. It matters about how it came to be. You were told she'd have to face up to what she's done and that is exactly what has happened," Samuel continued.

Astrid gave Samuel a perplexed look. He couldn't comprehend what Samuel was suggesting. Was he perhaps saying that Isra deserved what had occurred? No, that didn't make any logical sense at all. Who deserves to be taken away from everything they love; only to be sent tumbling down in some alternate reality as a result of things they did in the past?

In Astrid's mind, Isra had done some intolerable things that even he, in his good-natured ways, couldn't make head or tails of, but surely there was a kinder punishment than this. Being led off down the merry path into a catalytic Hell, being made to face up to every single wicked thing you did to another soul was too much.

"Are you saying she deserves it?" Astrid breathed. He sounded upset, almost whimpering. It was like he was dreading hearing something he really didn't want to know about.

"I'm saying what's done is done. She knows that. It doesn't matter what you believe. Every individual that comes into being with this earth, whether witch, mortal, or even a hearted fae, none let slip that there's a penalty for actions that go against the light, but they still know," Samuel chortled on, as if he was reciting some long-lost law that had been cast aside but suddenly, now he had a chance to regain his sense of knowing.

Astrid eyed Samuel carefully, checking to see if there was even one tiny sign that his old master might be lying. Whatever came out of his mouth in the next few seconds was imperative as to whether Astrid took matters into his own hands.

"Is she dead?" Astrid asked. He took a breath, allowing the air to filter through his lungs.

"No," Samuel answered.

He looked up to the ceiling for a moment as if in pause. Anything he said now could be disastrous. Samuel knew he would have to be sincere and straightforward with Astrid in order to guarantee he didn't lose his temper or at least safeguard against him totally flying off the handle.

"She won't be, not if you do what I say. I want you to get to her in time, but I don't want you unleashing bloodshed that will no doubt lead to ghastly peril for the boy, Astrid," Samuel insisted.

"I didn't say I was going to place my wrath upon him..." Astrid started and stopped. Defensiveness could be picked up in his voice.

Samuel smiled, remembering how well he knew Astrid. There was something else he wanted to say but didn't. It would take some gentle nudging to make him say it.

"But?" Samuel probed.

Astrid turned away toward the window, not wanting to give Samuel any indication of what he was thinking. *There are some things a man must keep to himself. I am a man. I have my principles and virtues. I believe this man should pay for his misjudgment. I'm not going to feel guilty for wanting to get my revenge on him.*

Astrid realized that his thoughts were likely being read so he turned to Samuel again. Their eyes met on a symmetrical level although Astrid was the first to break the contact, looking down at the floor.

"But nothing," Astrid replied as if in unison with Samuel's thoughts.

"No, you can do better than that," Samuel quipped. "I know there's something on your mind, so why don't you just get it out there."

Samuel's eyes were glued to Astrid's face, watching his hardened expression.

"But I think he should pay," Astrid blurted.

Astrid appeared to have no emotion at all. He was deadly serious. You could see the revenge was so tempting to him, it was practically beaming out from his eyeballs. The fixation of it pressed into Astrid's mind as if nothing else mattered other than dealing with Ronald in his very unique way.

Samuel unfolded his arms, glancing toward Ronald and then Astrid again. "There are other ways other than creating chaos in the form of death. As a lightbearer, I shouldn't have to remind you of that. You let the man go and I'll tell you where Isra is. You could be there before nightfall if you choose to let bygones be bygones where this individual is concerned."

Samuel was of course referring to Ronald, but was hoping Astrid was going to take heed of his reprimand. Astrid loosened a little. He didn't want to give up the idea of revenge but he had to admit that just being given Isra was better than never laying his eyes on her again. If it meant bargaining with Samuel over the life of another to save Isra, then golly he was prepared to do it.

"And what will you do with this vile piece of shit?" Astrid inquired. The anger emitted from his lips was like steam off a fire.

Ronald flashed an eye at Astrid upon hearing every word. "I am still here, you know," he muttered in the raven-man's direction.

"Shut your mouth. The fact you are here is enough to irritate me for several hundred lifetimes. Now be quiet and maybe you will get to see them," Astrid threatened.

Samuel resisted the urge to burst out laughing. He had to satisfy Astrid's curiosity though, just as an insurance policy to keep things neutral between them.

"I've been wanting a new familiar. I don't have a raven anymore. I haven't had one for quite some time," he said, winking at Astrid.

Astrid relented, dropping his shoulders. He swallowed his pride as he spoke. "All right. I'll let you have your wicked way with the boy. Now, will you tell me where I will find Isra?"

Samuel nodded, signaling to Ronald. "You're mine," he whispered in the terrified mortal's ear.

All Ronald could do was tremble as Samuel stood above him smug and in control, all the things that Ronald was not any longer.

"I'd rather tell you alone, dear son," Samuel muttered, pushing Astrid toward the door of the cottage. He opened it a little so that it was ajar. Samuel motioned over to Astrid, dragging him outside, for he wanted to say this quietly.

Astrid stood waiting for what Samuel had to say. He barely paid Ronald any attention. The idea of revenge seemed to have dissipated from his head. Samuel came up from behind, placing his lips next to Astrid's ear, taking care to make sure he would not be overheard. Astrid listened keenly as Samuel told him the sacred tidbit. A relaxed glow emitted from Astrid's soul as Samuel finished excreting the words.

Finally, after a moment, Astrid pulled away. Samuel turned to him warmly, patting him on the shoulder. "And remember, I don't want to hear of you doing anything that might cause animosity between us. You certainly don't want me showing up again in bad circumstances. It's been good seeing you, Astrid," Samuel said, watching Astrid walk away.

22

Astrid hurried on ahead, plundering through the forest.

He wasn't sure where his destination was, but Samuel had said that Astrid couldn't miss it even if he'd tried to. It was the golden acreage. Samuel had told Astrid it was a square of yellow-golden tones with bold red roses and deep purple ones scattered all over the place, a typical countryside setting packed with quaint charm.

Astrid had no inclination of the black rose, but as soon as Samuel had mentioned it, something inside Astrid hit a high note, like something he'd heard before but couldn't quite recollect where he had picked up its first appearance in his mind.

When Samuel had whispered to Astrid, he made things very clear. The black rose was a rare flower only deemed to show up when darkness was afoot. It was created for the very same reason and was designed to be in the golden field when Isra's fate collided with that of the prophecy he had told Astrid of three years earlier.

Astrid was silent as he trudged along, deep in contemplation over what he would do and say when he arrived at his fortuitous destination. Embarking on a journey like this wasn't new to Astrid as he had done so earlier on in the year to seek out whether Isra was, in fact, still immortal. And if she wasn't, he wanted to know if death could strike at her again.

He had never revealed the outcome of that trip to Isra, intentionally withholding what he had found out, but now he was thinking about that on a whole different level, remembering everything so clearly in the back of his mind as if it was yesterday.

~

"You know why I'm here," Astrid called out.

An elder woman stood behind him. Wafts of gray hair that had missed being tied into a tight bun floated around her face.

"Yes, I know. You want to know if your dear lady witch will succeed in defeating death if another attempt is made on her life," she said with caution.

Astrid felt awkward standing inside this cottage, feeling resentment coming at him from the old woman. He wasn't sure on why she didn't have a rapport with Lady Isra, but the tension coming from her in waves was deadly.

"Agnes, I'm not here to harm you or your clan. I just want what I came here for," he reassured her.

Agnes turned her head, looking at him in disbelief. She hastily managed a chuckle. "I should find this amusing to be asked to help the witch that took my dear Contessia, but my days of humor are long gone," she retorted with a sullen expression on her face.

"I understand. I play a part in that too, but Isra is someone I care about very deeply. I would be most grieved to lose her again," Astrid explained.

"I see your reasoning goes against my logic. I apologize. I have to say, this is a very difficult situation but, I must warn you that she's not out of the woods yet."

Astrid stared at Agnes. His entire mind worked at once to try and fathom what the old woman was saying to him. He couldn't understand whether she meant Isra would die again and this time forever, or whether she would be saved from fate's good graces once again.

"For a creature as wicked as your Isra, I must be clear when I state there is unfinished business coming her way and some things, such as the moon rising at night, cannot be stopped," Agnes muttered. The gaze in her warm eyes was serious.

"I don't understand," Astrid sputtered. He was anxious. His hands tensed as he struggled to stop his fidgeting fingers in panic.

"It's clear to me that she will meet with those she has destroyed again, but the feel of it is the powers that be are in charge here and they say she must face judgment for her actions." Agnes continued with her eyes closed, as if she was speaking from what she was seeing in her mind's eye. "There is something else, but it won't make her perish. It's just a lesson. A lesson we must all learn when we mess with forces that are beyond us."

She was wise as she said it, as if it were a prophecy that had been unraveled.

"But I can assure you it won't kill her. It's just the way the universe works with beings of her kind." Agnes snorted, though she wasn't amused. "I'm sorry it's not what you were wanting to hear, but I can only give you the truth of the matter. And the truth is, it's not over yet."

Astrid stood quietly, not wanting to look at Agnes for fear she might sense he was worried in his heart. He so badly didn't want to lose Isra again and certainly not to some prophesied event coming that nobody would be able to halt.

Astrid paused, the memory fading. He quickly realized where he was. A golden shimmer came into his vision. *Oh my, this must be it. The place Samuel was on about. The golden field. I just hope she's okay.*

He figured at this point, his thoughts weren't going to be overheard. Truthfully, he even felt a little reassured which is so unusual for a man so precarious over the unknown. All he'd have to do was discover her from the wretched place and then bring her home. That was all that was at the forefront of his mind, keeping him sharp and focused on the task ahead.

He edged closer to the meadow. Astrid marveled at how glorious it was. Sparkling sheen covered all of its acreage while undaunted roses spread out across its gold brilliance. Astrid began to push on, searching every inch of it for Isra. He hadn't managed to ascertain from Samuel's know-how exactly where Isra would be.

Plundering on into the depths of auroral land, seeming delirious as if it was something out of someone's fancy, he continued to walk through the auspicious pasture, not knowing just where it was going to end. Succulent blue flowers that hung off the ends of branches looking honeyed came out of the corner of his eye. Wow, it really was a candy-coated place of imagination. Like a child dipping their toe in pastel-colored waters, it promised joy and enchantment bigger than they could envision in their young minds.

Whatever it was, he aimed to get out of here, escaping with Isra in his arms very much alive. He had no time for a thoughtless daydreaming into fantasy.

Suddenly in the distance, a white shimmer caught his attention. He couldn't see what it was as it was too far away, but it was definitely something. Taking heed, he ran through masses of bright brassy blades until the white was in front of him.

Isra's hair spread out across the golden bank. Astrid stopped, kneeling down in front of her. She was still breathing but her eyes were closed. He lifted a stray hair covering her right eye. She was still, lying like porcelain, stiff and rigid. Although it was easy to tell she hadn't met mortal peril, Astrid took due care to ensure she was breathing in her transgression. For someone who had already tripped away from death once, it was remarkable to think she'd done it again, like a firefly whose glow had never weakened.

Without hesitation, he moved himself closer to her undisturbed body. A breath escaped him as his lips found hers. The skin on them was cold but still soft as he gently pressed his lips upon her. He whispered, "I think I know just how to break this spell," into her ear.

Closing his eyes in faith she would awake from this curse, he waited, keeping his eyes closed. Everything was silent within him as he bent down and kissed her. Nothing but silence followed. It was deafening. A crow could be heard cawing but not a single sound came from the quaint sleeping woman he knelt over.

"No. It can't be, no!" He wept into her hair. She showed no sign of life. He had dreaded this, the moment she wouldn't wake up. *Oh goodness, it can't be true,* he thought. *She just can't leave me like this.*

A coughing sound ensued. The sleeping body gasped!

Astrid opened his eyes in amazement. Isra's eyes met his, fluttering open. He rushed at once to hug her. His inviting arms almost crushed her bones in his excitement. Astrid embraced her. Lady Isra was his once again, safe in his arms. He was not going to let her go this time.

The End.

INTRODUCING DARKNESS REBORN
DARK SPELL SERIES BOOK 8

Lady Isra lay completely still on her bed with her eyes half-open. She was not asleep, but not totally awake either. It was almost as if she was in a meditative state, traveling to another land from the comfort of her warm, safe bed. This was ironic considering she had been in another desolate realm of darkness and death while her body lay sleeping for eons of time in the golden field.

But Isra had felt over-rested, so lying awake would suffice her needs for now. Time away from Astrid was wholly needed though she didn't come to the bedroom to sleep. She had slept an eternity away already.

When Isra had returned to Shambre Fell with Astrid, the atmosphere could have been cracked with a knife. He had kissed her and awoken her from Ronald's spell, but she had already been informed by both Everilda and Kane.

They went their separate ways. She retired to the bedroom while he sought solace in their grand throne room, probably brooding over everything he had done. And it wasn't that the relationship was over between them. Their love had not died and shriveled up. And no, Isra didn't hate him, but after Everilda's revelation and hearing the truth from two ghosts from her near distant past, things had felt awfully strained between them.

Isra now needed quiet time to mull over everything that had happened between them because finding out someone you love had been hiding something from you for two whole years was not something that was easy to sweep under the rug.

Isra needed the sanctuary of her space to figure it out. How she hadn't picked up on the signs was inconceivable to her. How was it possible that she didn't pick on Astrid's fiery anxiety that peaked whenever she was near him? Especially when Onyx crashed into the grand throne room, wailing like a banshee. Isra wondered if she was under Astrid's spell. Or more precisely, was she so in love with him, his deep magnetic heroic presence coated in deep-seated brooding, that she let her guard down allowing him to deceive her the way he had?

Either way, it didn't matter. She knew the truth now. The whole sordid truth. And as grotesque as it was, Isra understood Astrid's reasoning. She wasn't about to run out on him. She got him on a spiritual level and in turn, he did with her. Astrid got into the places of Isra that no man had ever been able to touch. Isra delved into all the aspects of how it had panned out. It wasn't that hard to fathom why Astrid took over Kane in that manner. He felt that by doing away with the boy, transforming him into a kitten, Kane would be unable to harm them. And he was right because Kane was totally helpless.

However, Isra had loved that sweet kitten Onyx from the moment she laid eyes on him. His death was something that had shaken her to almost rock bottom, causing her to flee from Astrid for the first time ever. But now she knew it was Kane. It wouldn't be easy to just slink away from that, not knowing all she knew now.

She had petted that sweet, furry head unaware it was that slithering, whimpering man hidden away in a furry suit. It was sickening to her. All that time, it had been Kane. When she had fed him and kissed him ... oh god, that was irksome to think about, for she had spent many sweet moments gushing over Onyx, cooing at him! It didn't even bear thinking about. Just the mere idea of it made her stomach turn.

It's absolutely vile at best, Isra thought to herself. *But no matter, we must move on.*

Isra let her head fall against the soft white pillow. It was a warm yet breezy winter day. The window was open just enough to let some icy cold air in. It was hard for Isra to believe winter had arrived already. She watched the snow gently fall from her bedside, her eyes closing as she began to drift off, remembering how Astrid had awakened her only twelve hours ago.

Astrid couldn't believe it. He was like an excited child. Those brown eyes were warm and full of glee. He was unable to contain his happy tears. They fell down his face like avalanches of joy.

"Isra," he gasped. "I can't believe it. I thought I had lost you. Again!" Astrid emphasized. He was remembering how she had died in his arms on that all too painful rainy night. It was only a year ago, but still the memory stabbed him right in his humanized heart.

"You won't ever lose me," Isra muttered. She attempted to lift herself up although it was a strain to even sit up from this affixed position she was in.

"No, don't try moving too quickly," Astrid warned her while also smiling.

He was practically beaming at her, just gently watching as Isra slowly adjusted to the world around her, although Isra was not smiling back at him. She seemed stiff and uncomfortable in his company for the first time ever. He had never witnessed her like this. She seemed cold and irrational in her manner.

"I want to go home," she announced formally to him. "Back to Shambre Fell."

"Okay," Astrid replied, taken aback at her.

I was hoping we could continue where we left out without this stuff surfacing out, he thought to himself. *I know I messed up. I know I played one hell of a masquerade here but believe me, I did it for you.*

"I know many things have happened in my absence," she breathed, eyeing him closely. It was like she was feeling her way through him, examining every facet of his being in this moment. "I am not trying to be awkward, but after resting for an eternity while taken down to a subliminal Hell-like place, I am not one for small talk at this time."

Astrid bent his head. The guilt crept up on him, sweeping over him like a tidal wave, soaking into every part of his soul. It was inevitable Isra would react like this when she finally discovered the truth and it was clear in her tone of voice that she knew.

"I understand, but I hope you don't hate me," Astrid admitted, reaching across for her hand, clutching it in his own cold hand like it was a hot coal full of heat and smoldered passion. "I cannot lose you," he whispered, looking up at her.

Isra smiled for the first time since awakening. "I know. You won't lose me. I just need time." She spoke with a solemn expression. "Just, let's go home, Astrid."

Astrid climbed onto her, taking care not to allow his weight to submerge her before pressing his lips onto her own in a passionate embrace. "I am so lucky to have ever laid eyes on you," he gushed.

Astrid's eyes beamed while his heart jumped inside his chest, gently slowing as he met her eyes with his own. A moment of pure happiness emitted from him.

"I never regretted my decision to come after you when I was warned not to, but even with the prophecy of the black rose, I still came crashing in like the knight I had always wanted to be, just with feathers," Astrid articulated, twirling one of his fingers through her luscious golden hair.

～

Isra was deep in sleep as the memory swept over her in her dream-like state. Smiling to herself as it unfolded, suddenly she was jerked awake by something landing on her bed with a thump. Anxious, she threw the covers off her with a start only to find a black raven looking up at her with a cheeky, crooked smile. A half-eaten worm dangled out of his mouth as if he had been recently enjoying the slimy offering. Isra felt relief, relaxing a little by sitting herself up.

"Silas!" she exclaimed. "I thought you were an intruder."

Silas bent his head down apologetically. "I am sorry. I should have made myself more known. Anyway, enough of the formalities. I wanted to ask how you were," Silas asked, looking guilt-ridden as he was the one that had not assisted Astrid in finding her sooner.

"I am afraid the blame lies with me for Astrid not getting to you quicker than he had. I had refused to help him," Silas explained, lifting his left wing up as if in mid-stretch. "You see, my brother has done some terrible things in his time, always getting into one scrape or another, and I was always the one that helped him out of it. This time I refused to do that. I told him it was time he corrected his own mistakes. I know it was harsh of me, but if I had known better, I would have sought to find you myself."

"It is all right, Silas," Isra comforted him. "You only did what you deemed right."

Silas seemed grateful for her understanding but still, something inside him felt off. He hated making a choice then finding out something much more ghastly could have commenced as a result of him making that choice. Silas lowered his wing once more before moving toward Isra. He found a comforting spot just below her thighs, perching on her leg.

"Yes, but I still regret it and for the issues my wrong doing caused. I do wholeheartedly apologize," he affirmed to her.

Isra smiled at him, patting his head. Her fingers glided down his soft black feathers, gently stroking him. "You are a good soul, Silas. You cannot fix everything in Astrid's life. You just simply cannot be that for him. Even he knows that, deep down," she asserted.

"Yes, well I do agree with that, but I still feel bad at how it went down, you know? One minute I hear you've been taken by that mortal ... and the next? Well, it doesn't bear thinking about. Here you are, a powerful witch in possession of powers most couldn't dream of, and you were carefully lured away by a treacherous trick from someone who wanted to place their blood-soaked wrath upon you," Silas explained in a serious tone. "And worse so, this man had enacted a deed much worse to your own and still couldn't see the light of what was right and good," he added solemnly.

There was a pause in the air. Nothing was said for a moment. It was just Silas and Isra looking at each other with plain, emotionless expressions. Both seemed to be reading into the other's thoughts as their eyes twitched at the same time. An acknowledgement of the existence of one good friend to another, their minds met up in the aftermath of chaos and bloodshed, merging into one. Warm smiles in reciprocation indicated mutual heartfelt feelings as both souls connected in the brief timeless moment, fleeting as they both shifted their eyes away, unable to stop the need to blink.

"You know, don't you?" Silas realized without hesitation.

Silas's eyes narrowed at Isra. Those warm black holes of mysticism and wonder seemed to go on for eons as he stared into her ones of bold, magnificent emerald green. *Oh she knows, all right. This is a woman that isn't afraid to delve into the dark. She knows every gritty, terrifying aspect of him. Isra isn't a fool. She was bound to uncover the deceit sooner or later,* Silas thought to himself.

Isra lowered her gaze with a furrowed brow. "Oh yes, I know. Having the man I mentally mind-fucked reveal Astrid's sordid little secret while being held hostage in another realm was not on my to-do list," she muttered sarcastically. "But still, I'm here to tell the tale which is more than I can say for Kane."

Silas nodded his head in acknowledgement. He had to admit looking at Isra, after all she had been through, she was looking mighty fine. Maybe there was some weakness that showed when she moved her legs or shifted her upper body to become more comfortable, but otherwise she had come through almost untouched.

"You are a fine woman, Isra. How you tolerate my brother is beyond me, but at least I can see the devotion you have for him. That's enough to tell me you won't cast him aside if he crosses the line..." Silas trailed off, quickly realizing Astrid had already done that and here Isra was standing by him.

Wow, she has some gusto. Silas thought to himself with a chuckle. *But I do secretly wonder whether she will dish out her own form of punishment? Still, it's not my business.*

Silas finished his train of thought, glancing back toward Isra with a cheeky smile. Silas's smile was enough to make Isra fall for his wayward charms and warped sense of humor that normally had them in hysterics with uncontrollable laughter. Isra lowered her gaze a little, those piercing green eyes of hers just about reaching the same level as Silas's head and with a fixated grin she replied.

"Because I love him."

"I know. Anyway, it's not my business. I just hope things are back to normal around here," Silas hinted, giving Isra a wink. "I must depart, I am afraid. I can't stay for too long. Astrid relies on me too much and it's time he stood on his own claws, well, footing. Still, I am so pleased you are well, Isra. I do hope you wouldn't mind me dropping in on occasion as I do miss our chats, as few as they were," Silas expressed.

"Of course, you are always welcome," Isra replied, extending her arm to Silas.

"Well, I must bid you *adieu*," Silas remarked, lifting his wings in anticipation.

"Yes, as must I," Isra whispered, watching Silas fly out of the open window. "I have an old friend to pay homage to." She smiled to herself once again.

But unbeknownst to Isra, there was someone lurking behind her bedroom door, keeping themselves hidden and quiet, out of the way while having been an eavesdropper in the conversation Isra and Silas had shared. The familiar face resisted the urge to cough, sneakily backing away a few paces in the knowing Isra was about to step out at any moment.

It was then that the person revealed themselves. That short, black hair now showed strands of gray as the stress had weathered him over the past few days. The muscular frame showed signs of way too much caffeine consumption and the warm brown eyes showed hurt resounding inside. It was none other than Astrid, quickly moving down the cold, stone steps to avoid being spotted by her or anyone for that matter.

"I wonder who she is paying homage to," Astrid said to himself as he reached the bottom of the stairs, dashing across the hallway as he disappeared out of sight.

DARK SPELLS READING ORDER

1. Her Dark Love
2. Kissing Darkness
3. Seducing Darkness
4. Queen of Darkness
5. Her Dark Soul
6. Her Dark Heart
7. Her Dark Rose
8. Darkness Reborn

ABOUT THE AUTHOR

USA Today Best Seller Isra Sravenheart resides in the UK. She is an avid reader, particularly in the fantasy and paranormal genres, and very much into all things fairytale and dark in nature. She is also a witty wordsmith.

Isra is known for being obsessed with coffee and very particular towards cats of which she owns four of the buggers.

You can follow Isra through her blog, or any of these social media platforms:

ALSO BY ISRA SRAVENHEART

The Dark Spell Series: Books 1 through 8

Heart of Oz

Tainted Siren

The Divine Spiritual Truth: A Twinflame Romance

DARK SPELL – BOOK SEVEN

HER DARK

ROSE

ISRA
SRAVENHEART

USA TODAY BEST-SELLING AUTHOR

www.ingramcontent.com/pod-product-compliance
Lightning Source LLC
Chambersburg PA
CBHW070353200726
48294CB00003B/892